UNCORRECTED PAGE PROOF

The Heart's Desire

a novel

Nahid Rac

ISBN: 0-87286-304-2 $18.95 (cloth)
ISBN: 0-87286-305-0 $8.95 (paper)

Pages: 208

Publication Date: October 1995

For additional information, contact:
Stacey Lewis
City Lights Books
(415) 362-1901

10 9 8 7 6 5 4 3 2 1

Cover design by Rex Ray
Book design by Nancy J. Peters
Typesetting by Harvest Graphics

Library of Congress Cataloging in Publication Data

City Lights Books are available to bookstores through our primary distributor: Subterranean Company, P.O. Box 160, 265 S. 5th St., Monroe, OR 97456. 503-847-5274. Toll-free orders 800-274-7826. FAX 503-847-6018. Our books are also available through library jobbers and regional distributors. For personal orders and catalogs, please write to City Lights Books, 261 Columbus Avenue, San Francisco, CA 94133.

CITY LIGHTS BOOKS are edited by Lawrence Ferlinghetti and Nancy J. Peters and published at the City Lights Bookstore, 261 Columbus Avenue, San Francisco, CA 94133.

For my sisters
Pari, Manijeh, Feri, ZiZi

Ah, Love! could thou and I with Fate conspire
To grasp this sorry Scheme of Things entire,
Would not we shatter it to bits—and then
Re-mould it nearer to the Heart's Desire!

Omar Khayyám

Chapter 1

Where am I? Jennifer sat up abruptly, naked, in the blue, mosaic-covered bathtub. Oh, I must have dozed off. I'm in my mother-in-law's house in Teheran. She had an unsettling feeling of being exposed. It was like the recurring nightmare she used to have as a girl, in which she would find herself in a classroom or on the street without her blouse on. She got out of the tub quickly and began to dry herself and dress.

Then she went into the bedroom and checked on her six-year-old son, Darius. It worried her that he was sleeping so long. Then she thought, he's probably still worn out from days of traveling. They'd gone from Athens, Ohio, to the Columbus airport, from there to JFK, then to Istanbul, where they had finally boarded Iran Air for Teheran. Then there was the long wait on the customs line in Mehrabad Airport, where all the suitcases had been virtually dumped out on the ground to be searched.

Through the tiny window she could see the sycamore trees lining the alley, scrawny, shriveled up, and the water in the *joob,* down to a narrow flow. It was unusually hot even for June. She thought of how magical Karim's homeland had been on their first visit twelve years ago, not long after they were married. Teheran had been exciting to explore, a huge and hectic city with ancient bazaars that sold jewelry, carpets, ceramics, as well as modern shops carrying the latest European fashions, a city where mosques and shrines stood next to nightclubs, traditional houses side by side with high-rises, where women walked on the streets in chadors or in bold miniskirts and low-cut blouses. The mosques, shrines, and steep stone stairways leading to underground wells had layers of history beneath them.

This ancient house itself, full of hallways and rooms, had fascinated her then. Several of the rooms had fireplaces decorated with stone friezes of fruit, flowers, animals, and cherubs with round, smiling faces, painted pink and blue and yellow. Many of the windows glowed with amber and red stained-glass panels. One of the rugs on the living room floor looked like a forest with pale green leaves scattered on it, another looked like a map of a city.

But now, in 1989, everything in Iran was touched by the tragedy of a prolonged eight-year war between Iran and its neighbor Iraq, which had ended only months ago. Though the fighting had gone on mainly around the western border, bombs had left their marks everywhere—you couldn't miss the charred window frames and boarded-up doors, the families camping in quiet back streets, soldiers passing by on crutches. Hundreds of thousands of Iranians, many of them mere teenage boys, only seven or eight years older than Darius, had been killed and wounded in the war. Black flags hanging on almost every door designated that someone in the household had been martyred. On the main square was a fountain with dark red water surging up from it. She had gasped when Karim told her it was meant to be a reminder of the blood shed. Even street names had been changed to point to the war: Martyrdom Street, Army Avenue, War Alley.

There were other changes too. Before the war, Iran had been through a revolution. After the shah left and Kohmeini came to power, there had been a severing of diplomatic relations with many countries, including the United States. Conditions for women had become more restrictive. They had to cover up thoroughly in the presence of men other than close relatives; many were expelled from their jobs. As a part of the effort to get rid of "vices," no American or European movies were allowed to be shown in cinemas, the nightclubs had been shut down, and Burger King and Kentucky Fried Chicken restaurants no longer existed. Not that she had come all the way to Iran to find American fast food—it was more that the climate was now inhospitable to her as an American, and worse, an American woman.

Her friends, when she had told them she was planning a two-month trip to Iran, had cautioned her against going—it could be dangerous for an American woman. When she had called the State Department to ask about the visa situation the woman answering the phone had said, "We have no embassy there, you're taking a risk to go." Indeed the process of getting in and out of Iran did involve a certain amount of risk. To travel to Iran she and Darius, though they were born in America, had to obtain Iranian passports through the Algerian Embassy in Washington, which represented Iranian interests in the United States. Then they had to stop off in Istanbul and hide their American passports in a bank safe; otherwise, if the passports were found on them in Iran, they would be confiscated. On the way back they would have to pick up their American passports again in Turkey.

But these were minor difficulties compared to the problem of Karim.

Ever since the trouble began between the two countries, a surge of hostility had risen in America toward Iranians. First it had been a blow to Karim when Iranian students were deported from the United States. For weeks, months, he could not stop talking about the unfairness of it, though he had no students from Iran himself. Then when Iran took the Americans as hostages, Iranians were caricatured, ridiculed in the press. A number of brutal incidents were reported in the local Athens paper. Even long after the hostages were released, prejudice against Iranians still lingered.

At first it seemed that these events had no effect on the bond between her and Karim, but as time passed she began to feel an invisible barrier growing between them. He often seemed lost, and alone. Lonely with her. She sometimes saw in his eyes a hint of accusation, "You don't understand." He acted, she felt, as if having been born in America gave her an advantage over him. She remembered a certain look he'd had one day, and that image of him often came into her mind; he was standing by the living room window, staring into the backyard of their house in Athens. "I'm never going to be happy here again," he had muttered. "Karim, don't say things like that," she had replied. He turned around and looked at her in a startled way as if unaware that he was speaking aloud.

She was hoping that this trip to Iran, a stay with his family, would provide a congenial atmosphere for him, would give him a new perspective. In fact it would be beneficial for all of them to spend some time in Iran. Darius would see where his father came from, get to know his grandmother. She and Karim would be in a new environment, away from all the tension and conflicts forced on them. It would be good for Karim, who was a professor of urban planning at Ohio University, and looked forward to being in Iranian cities again. And she could get ideas and inspiration from Persian art for her work as a graphic designer. When the cease-fire between Iran and Iraq went into effect, she was the one who suggested that they take the trip, and of course Karim himself had been waiting for the first opportunity.

A muezzin's voice calling people to prayers suddenly flowed out from a mosque. "Allaho Akbar . . ." Then she heard Karim's voice above that, "Jennifer, dinner will get cold."

She checked on Darius again and decided to let him sleep. She went to the courtyard, where the others—Karim; his mother, Aziz; Aziz's brother, Jamshid; Jamshid's wife, Monir; and their two teenage daughters, Zohreh and Azar—were sitting cross-legged on a rug under a tree. Food was arranged on a cloth spread between them. Jamshid, Karim had told her, had lost his engineering job in the oil refinery in Abadan because of the war and he was trying to relocate his family in Teheran. It's odd that Karim did not mention that all these relatives would be staying here. Did he know? So much went unsaid between them these days.

She sat cross-legged on the rug with the others and they began to eat—chicken kebab, spiced with turmeric and lemon, saffron rice, a stew, salad with lemon and herb dressing, *doogh*.

"Darius has been sleeping for hours," Aziz said, touching Karim's arm, her eyes intense, a little anxious.

In a loosely cut brown dress, her gray hair pulled back in a tight knot, wearing a simple gold ring with a carnelian stone, she projected plainness, austerity, Jennifer thought. Slightly arthritic, she wore thick black stockings in spite of the heat. She had not looked so severe on their first visit. Perhaps it was the strain of the war, her brother losing his job, the tragedies all around her. "Maybe I should wake him up?" she asked.

"Let him sleep, no harm," Karim said.

Suddenly the lights went out.

"Oh, no, I can't stand it any more! No electricity in a country rich with oil!" Zohreh, the older of the two sisters, said, looking at Jennifer with a smile as if to apologize.

Jennifer smiled back. She liked Zohreh, feeling a stronger connection with her already, in the few days they had been there, than with anyone else in Karim's family. She was a lively and curious young girl, and asked Jennifer many questions about America. She marveled at how well Jennifer spoke Farsi, which Jennifer was proud to have mastered over the years of her marriage.

"What do you expect? America caused this war, kept it going, and who knows what they'll do next . . ." Jamshid said. Then his voice got lost in Zohreh's and Azar's cheering cries as the lights came back on. In a moment he went on, "They should try to solve their own problems first before interfering with others. With all their wealth they haven't gotten rid of their social problems, loneliness, crime, poverty."

A wave of pain, mixed with shame, went through Jennifer. Of course there was reason for Iranians' anger and mistrust of America, she thought. America did exploit Iran as much as possible for its oil, then provided Iraq with arms to defeat the new government. At the same time, though, she resented Jamshid's attitude. It was as if he were attacking her personally.

"But the freedom they have there," Zohreh began.

"I don't want to give you a sociology lesson, but that's an illusion," her father interrupted with chagrin. "You ought to find a book called *The Lonely Crowd*, it will explain everything to you." He put down his fork and stood up. Leaning against a tree, he took out a cigarette from a silver case and lit it with a silver lighter.

Both the case and the lighter were from Tiffany's, Jennifer noticed. He was also wearing the Phi Beta Kappa key that he must have kept from his student days in Texas. He hasn't changed much, she thought, he's still vain and arrogant, particularly when talking to a woman—as hard to take as when he had visited them years ago in Ohio. She was not sure how she was going to live in close proximity with him in this house for two whole months.

Aziz and Monir began to clear the dishes, and Zohreh and Azar joined them. Jennifer did not offer to help this time—every time she had offered, Aziz had said, "Please sit down, you're a guest!" Jennifer could not quite understand Aziz's reactions and thoughts, was not sure if Aziz was being hospitable or if she did not trust her competence in domestic matters. After Aziz and Monir and her daughters had taken all the dishes into the kitchen, they came out with platters of fruit and nuts and arranged them on the cloth.

"I wish there was something to do at night," Zohreh said, again glancing at Jennifer, as if she were saying it for her benefit. Then she got up and went to her room, so did her sister. In a moment the sound from a radio drifted into the courtyard. A woman was singing, "Truth is like a flowing river, elusive, hard to hold."

Chapter 2

Jennifer lay awake in bed while Karim sat in the courtyard talking to his uncle, hanging on his words, laughing at his jokes. It was hard to fall asleep with all the sounds that carried over from the courtyard and other bedrooms—Zohreh and Azar shared one room, Jamshid and Monir another, and Aziz had one to herself. The heat was not helping. The ceiling fan had stopped turning because the electricity had gone off again and, with only one window, there was no ventilation. But mainly what kept her up was her own churning thoughts. Was the trip going to resolve anything? As Karim became enveloped in the circle of his family, he grew only more distant from her. And she was worried about Darius—he just wasn't himself. He was listless, homesick. Though he was picking up the language a little, building on the bit of knowledge of it he had already, he still could not understand most of what went on around him. There were no children his own age he could play with. He had been asking constantly, "Mommy, when are we going home?"

Her watch read 1:00 A.M., Iran time, seven and a half hours later than in Ohio. Their best friends, Nancy and Don, would be eating dinner. It was only five days ago that they had driven them to the airport, but it seemed much longer somehow. Darius missed their son, Josh, with whom he played almost every day.

She remembered admiring the watch, an oval-shaped Concord with golden hands and a tiny sapphire on the stem, in the window of a jewelry store in Columbus. Just when she had forgotten about it Karim had brought it home to her. It was his first birthday present to her, twelve years ago. It had been so good between them then. Being with him in the seclusion of a room, hearing him speak Farsi, his melodic language (the alphabet, the musical sounding words, were like symbols in a dream), or looking at his face, outlined by the mass of his dark hair, his eyes beaming with warmth, used to make her feel an intense, inexplicable happiness. It was as if he connected with something in a deep recess of her unconscious. Growing up in Margaretville, a small, farming town in upstate New York, she had envisioned traveling one day to countries where the way of life was different from her own. When she was a teenager, on days off from school she would go with her father to Kingston, where he was an electrician, and spend the day reading in the library—novels with foreign settings were her favorites. She thought of that dreamy moment of meeting Karim. It was in the cafeteria of Ohio State University in Columbus, where they were both students. He had picked up the fork she had dropped and replaced it with another one for her; then he had stared into her eyes. "Your eyes are an incredible color," he had said, so naturally that it had not sounded like a line. They had started going out and never stopped. He was always so intense and involved with whatever issue they talked about. They had two weddings. First they were married by a justice of the peace with only two of their friends present as witnesses. But a few months later, when they were planning their trip to Iran, they had been married by a Moslem priest—a Moslem wedding certificate was required for her to go to Iran as Karim's wife. She had stood next to Karim, her arms clasped in his, while the *aghound* said some words in Arabic and they repeated them. Then the *aghound* had given her the name Zahra. For her the sheer exoticness of the event had filled the air with a delicate sensuality. She felt perversely liberated. "Call me Zahra tonight," she would say playfully to Karim sometimes and tried to imagine how a true Moslem wife would behave. More passionate, more passive? She had asked Karim, "How does a Moslem wife act, tell me." He said, laughing, "How do I know, I've never been married to one. You're the first!"

She was finally falling asleep when she heard Karim undressing in the dark, then going over to Darius to check on him. In a moment he came to bed and lay next to her. She put her arm around his waist. He turned over and kissed her neck, cheek, lips. He caressed her thighs, breasts. The physical passion was still so alive between them in spite of everything . . .

He stopped suddenly, perhaps thinking of Darius in the room.

"Good night," he said and turned away.

In the morning, after breakfast, Karim suggested that the three of them go out and do some exploring. As she put on the chador, Jennifer recalled a conversation she had had with Nancy.

"Are you going to wear the *chador* in Iran?" Nancy had asked.

"I like the idea of trying it, to see how it feels."

"But the principle of it, to be *forced*," Nancy had said.

It was one thing to imagine wearing it and another to do it day after day, Jennifer thought.

"Why do you have to wear that on your head all the time?" Darius asked her, full of questions.

"It's the law here," Karim answered for her.

"Daddy, why don't *we* cover ourselves up?"

"I'll explain it to you some other time," Karim said, smiling.

As they were leaving the house, Jennifer was aware of surprised glances from everyone in the family, as if something strange were happening, as if they were being left out.

They walked down the alley to Jamali Avenue and waited for a taxi. Taxis were very cheap in Iran, no more than the bus fare in Ohio, a real asset, Jennifer thought, considering how hard it was to figure out the complicated bus routes. Several taxis went by without responding to Karim's raised hand. The heat was intense and it was dusty from lack of rain. Rain was so scarce in the summer that windshield wipers were removed from cars. The trees lining the streets were withered, and the Alburz Mountains in the distance had a brown, arid look. But traffic went by at its usual hectic pace, cars, mainly Iranian-made Paykans, pickup trucks, buses, motorscooters, motorcycles, bicycles, all competing to get ahead, even through red lights. The air was filled with their noise and fumes from their exhaust pipes and the dust rising from the unpaved parts of the ground. Amid the heavy traffic a man was riding a donkey. A group of men in threadbare gray clothes, clearly out of work, were standing next to a row of carpet shops as if hoping for something to come their way. Not far from the shops stood a hospital for disabled veterans, it seemed, judging by the number of men on crutches walking around in its garden. With all that went the jumbled shouts of peddlers, vendors, who displayed their merchandise on cloths they had spread on the sidewalk or on carts. "Only ten *toomans* for a skewer." "Fresh pecans, a bag for only five *toomans*." "The best ice-cream sandwich, come closer and see for yourself." "The best leather in the city . . ."

"Let's go to the Islamic Museum first," Karim said. "It's not far. We went there last time we were here—it was called Shahi Museum then."

She remembered it well. There had been an excited energy between Karim and her then. They had gazed at each miniature painting, some with dragons in the clouds or faces in rocks and he had told her what he knew about each piece. She had gotten ideas for her work from the exhibition. One pattern she had drawn for Design Loft, the company she worked for in Columbus, was inspired by one of the paintings, a motif of white cumulus clouds against a blue background. Another one that the director had liked was also inspired by a painting there—blue birds sitting among pink roses and pale green branches.

Finally a taxi stopped and they got in. It moved very slowly, the traffic was so heavy. When they reached the museum, there was a note on the door, "Closed For Repairs."

"So this is out for today," Karim said.

"We could go to the Carpet Museum."

"I don't want to have to wait for a taxi again." He thought for a moment. "There's a little shrine, not far from Teheran we could go to by train. The station is only a few blocks away."

A demonstration was going on as they headed toward the station. Knots of people were standing in doorways and on sidewalks or were leaning out of windows and balconies and watching. Karim picked Darius up in his arms and they tried to find their way through the crowd. The air was throbbing with the hum of people repeating over and over, "Down with America . . ." "Down with the Great Satan, the Mercenary America!"

"What are they saying, Mommy?" Darius asked.

"America and Iran are mad at each other."

"I don't want them to be mad," he said.

"We don't either, honey," Karim said. "But sometimes these things can't be helped."

The train to Shah Abdul Azim was old and bumpy. Darius laid his head on Jennifer's arm and looked out quietly. In about an hour the train came to a stop. They got out and went through a small bazaar. Karim bought a clay donkey and a pinwheel for Darius. They came out of the bazaar and started to walk through several interlocking courtyards. In one, a man was cutting inscriptions on gravestones, in another, families were sitting in the shade of ancient, dusty sycamore and cypress trees, picnicking. Mullahs in long khaki-colored robes walked by. Old men sat against the walls, one in the hollow of a tree, staring into space. Pigeons fluttered on the ornate parapets on rooftops. An old man, thin and gnarled, holding a parrot on his index finger, came up and stood against a tree and people began to collect around him. The parrot said over and over, "Hello, how are you on this fine day?"

Finally they reached the shrine. Through the entrance door Jennifer could see the room inside, a dazzling sight, with the walls covered by hundreds of tiny mirrors, rimmed with gold, masses of silver inlaid between them. People were leaning against the walls and kissing the silver.

They checked their shoes and started to go in. She became aware of the guard's scrutinizing gaze on her.

He asked Karim, "Is she a Moslem?"

It must be my blue eyes and maybe the way I hold the chador, Jennifer thought. He knows I'm foreign.

"Yes," Karim said.

"Is she your wife?"

Karim nodded.

"Do you have proof?"

"Not with me, why would I?"

"We need proof," the man said, turning away and attending to someone else.

"I'm sorry," Karim said to her as they turned around to leave. "But it won't do us any good to argue with him. Why don't we have some lunch and then just go home. We can come back here another day and bring proof."

They started walking back to the bazaar. Jennifer was aware of the chador weighing heavily on her head.

Chapter 3

After eating in a hot little chelo kebab restaurant, they caught the next train back to Teheran.

When they got home no one was in the courtyard. Darius wandered to his grandmother's room and Jennifer and Karim went into theirs. He pulled the shade over the window and latched the door from the inside, then they both undressed and got into bed. They began to kiss and caress with urgency—with awareness, on his part too, she knew, that their time alone together in the room was brief. They skipped the preliminaries. His lips on hers only for a moment, he was already hard, moving inside her. They were pushing for the peak quickly. Karim breathed heavily and pulled out of her.

Then they lay there, holding each other. Karim seemed pensive.

"Remember you used to say it doesn't matter where we are as long as we're together?" he said. "You didn't know, and I didn't either, what would happen."

There was something ambiguous about his tone. "What do you mean?" she asked.

"You know how hard it is for me there now, and it's no easier for you here." He took a strand of her hair and pushed it behind her ear. He embraced her tightly, but the dark shadow was there between them.

"We're sleeping on the bed you slept on as an adolescent. Doesn't that feel good?"

He was quiet.

"What is it?" she asked.

"I just regret that my mother wasn't with us at the crucial times of my life—at our wedding, at Darius's birth."

"I know, but we came here right after the wedding and when Darius was born there was the war, she couldn't get out."

"It isn't just that," Karim said. "My family has been immersed in so much tragedy. Poor Jamshid losing his job, his home."

"But at least the war is over now, and as your mother keeps saying, thank God we're all healthy." She paused. "Honestly, Karim, would you like to live here now?"

"It's a complicated question."

"We could at some point, maybe when your sabbatical comes up in four years. I could try to arrange with the company to do some of my work here. I could take some courses in Persian art too, I'd love that."

"Four years, it's so long," he said sounding more resigned than argumentative.

"Karim, Karim . . ." Jamshid was calling.

Karim jumped out of the bed and began to put on his clothes quickly.

Jennifer was aware of a keen loneliness as Karim almost ran out of the room to respond to his uncle. She thought again of how close she had been once to this man from so far away and with him now in the room of his childhood she felt they were each being pulled in opposite directions.

But then, she thought, her loneliness had begun months before this trip, back when Karim had begun to act strangely. He sought out anything Iranian, a mosque, newspapers printed in Farsi, occasional radio programs in Farsi. He looked for other Iranians. At first he had become friends mainly with two Iranian men who also were married to American women. The six of them got together as couples. The new friendships were interesting in some ways. She loved the Persian food that the other two Iranian men cooked—lamb marinated in yogurt, rice in a mound on a platter with saffron coloring the top layer. Karim had started to do some Persian cooking too when they had invited those couples over to their house. She liked hearing about the experiences the men had had growing up in Iran and then as foreign students in America. But there was always a strain. The two wives, both younger than she, were even more bewildered than she was by their husbands' sudden obsessive preoccupation with Iran. "There was a time when no one even knew or cared where Iran was," one of them said.

Gradually, as the relationship among the men grew more intense, the women were excluded. Other Iranian men, some unmarried, joined the group. Karim began to put himself at their service almost as if he had pledged a fraternity. Whenever they called, he dashed out no matter what time it was or what else he had planned to do. He and the rest of them had started growing beards at the same time. They went to Columbus together to eat in an Iranian restaurant and then to a mosque where someone was giving a talk about Iran. Sometimes they went on hikes together. They sat up late into the night and read to each other from Iranian books and newspapers. On the anniversary of a martyr's death, they had a lamb slaughtered and gave the meat to Meals on Wheels.

His friends' needs had begun to come before hers and sometimes even Darius's. Just this past year Karim had missed Darius's birthday party to be with one of them. "He needs me to stay with him, he's very upset, his cousin died from wounds he got in the war." It was reasonable, if it had not been a part of a pattern. And it was unprecedented for him to miss Darius's birthday. Their son's birth had been a great event in their lives, particularly because for a long time she had had trouble conceiving.

Darius had been withdrawn at the party despite all the children; the bright decorations, streamers, and balloons Jennifer had hung on the walls; and the games she had arranged for them to play. He moved, touched things distractedly, asked elliptical questions. Nancy, who had come over to help, had said to Jennifer, "You know, he's upset because his father isn't here . . ."

At last even the web of Iranian friends around Karim could not seem to mitigate his feelings of dislocation. Sometimes she woke in the middle of the night and found him sitting in the living room watching television or reading.

The first few times she had gotten up to go to him. "Karim, you couldn't sleep? What's wrong?"

"You know . . . it must be the darkness, it makes everything seem even worse than it is."

"But what's upsetting you?"

"Nothing, nothing."

"Please tell me," she asked, her stomach churning with a sense of foreboding.

"I just feel lonely."

"What about Darius and me?" she asked.

"When I'm home, with you and Darius, I'm all right, but it's like being on an island . . ."

As time went by, that look of, "You don't understand," appeared more frequently on his face.

When he first came to the United States, he had gone to college in San Diego, then to Ohio State to study urban planning. He had tried to know the American culture as fully as he could. When they had just met he had told her he didn't approve of other Iranians who isolated themselves. More than once he had said, "I came here to get educated and then return home and put it into practice, but now I can't give up what I have here." He had made what seemed to be irrevocable choices. He had married her, an American woman, took on a full-time job at an American university, became an American citizen.

Karim's voice in the courtyard saying something in an agitated way to his uncle shook her out of her thoughts.

Then Karim dashed into the room. "A letter from Ed

Clancy," he said. "They've hired someone else in my field." He handed an envelope to her. "Read it."

She threw on a robe, took the letter out of the envelope and began to read it, filled with a sense of foreboding.

Dear Karim,

I thought you'd like to know that we have hired Jim Bower as an assistant professor to work with us, starting this fall. As you recall he was among the three we invited to apply to the department. He took his time and we had almost given him up but then he called last week and accepted the position.

She looked up at him. What was wrong? "It sounds like it's something you knew about."

"Did you read the whole letter?"

She read on.

To get him to come—I hope you don't mind this—we promised he could teach your seminar on urban infrastructure. We put your name down for the Intro course instead. Between you and me your trip to Iran has put the department in an awkward position. I'm concerned that you may not be able to come back on time, considering the instability and unpredictability in the Gulf.

Regards, Ed

Blood drained from her face. The letter sounded cold, impersonal, Ed didn't even bother asking how they were. Now that she thought about it, the few times she had seen Ed recently at departmental affairs he had been reserved, and once—very upsetting to Karim—he had invited several people from the department to dinner and had not included Karim and her. Still, she thought Karim overreacted to everything, took every gesture and word from Ed as an insult. "Ed is probably just looking after his own interests," she said. "Nothing directly against you, I'm sure."

"Oh, no? It's my course they've given to Bower without even consulting me. And you know something, this was mailed two weeks ago, before we had even left for Iran. He clearly didn't want to talk about it with me in person."

"It's only just one course." She tried to calm him. "I know it's more Ed's attitude. . . ."

But he grabbed the letter from her hand, and crumpled it up. "You don't understand . . ." Now he said what his eyes had already expressed.

He threw the letter on the floor and left the room. She sat on the bed, faint with despair.

Finally she decided to call Nancy. Don, Nancy's husband, who taught in the physics department, knew Ed and other members of Karim's department. Maybe she could get an objective reaction from them.

Anyway she had been longing to talk to Nancy, she hoped she could get through—the telephone lines in Iran were almost always out of order because of unrepaired war damage.

Nancy was taking care of their mail and watering their plants while they were away. She worked in Columbus too, as an editor for a nature magazine. Her son Josh was Darius's age, and they often got together with the children. Nancy usually came to their house, in a secluded neighborhood tucked away behind the university. On nice days Josh and Darius would go across the street and play in the field or watch the freight train, hooting and whistling by, on the tracks on the other side. On stormy days they might stay indoors and have coffee and hot chocolate, listening to the rain drum on the roof. On weekends one of the women would call the other, "Why don't you come over for dinner? I'll make something easy," or, "I invited the Porters over for brunch on Sunday, would you come too?" Don and Karim enjoyed debating various issues, discussing their work. Sometimes they stayed up late into the night talking. But then, when Karim started to spend more and more time with other Iranians, he saw less and less of Don.

Next to her address book, Jennifer found a sheet of paper on which Darius had drawn a picture with crayons. It was of a two-story house, shingled, set on a tree-filled street, their house in Athens, Ohio. She had been repainting Darius's room before they left. He had wanted his room yellow, like Josh's room.

She put down the drawing, sat on a chair next to the phone, and gave the number to the operator.

"I'll be happy to try for you, but it's nearly impossible to get through," the operator said. There was a pause as she made the connection, followed by a recorded message, "Calls are temporarily limited due to equipment problems. Please place your call again."

"Damn!" Jennifer slammed down the heavy, black phone.

Chapter 4

Karim accompanied his uncle to a job interview and then they went to a café to unwind before going home. But even in the presence of his uncle, sitting in this pleasant outdoor café set on a platform over a stream, with the sound of the water gurgling underneath them, he could not shake off the feeling Ed's letter had evoked.

"They're mediocre and smug," he said. "All the showing off about work and research, fights over secretaries' time, over space, all the politicking . . ."

"Do you think . . ." Jamshid paused to light a cigarette. He started again, "Would you want to look into a job here in Iran? So many qualified people have fled the country. And, believe it or not, an American degree is still what they trust the most here."

"It would be very hard for Jennifer here," Karim said. "And Darius too. . . . He's just a child though, he'd adjust."

"You stayed in the United States for years, you could ask her to stay here for a while."

Karim felt a sudden tension, talking about Jennifer to his uncle. He just said, "The truth is there's nothing there for me to go back to." Ed's behavior was only touching other, deeper wounds, Karim thought, drifting away into himself. How dislocated he had begun to feel in his own house, neighborhood. Dislocated, unwelcome, misunderstood, the target of all sorts of prejudices and hostilities. "Go Home! Go Home!" was written on walls. Once they had driven to the Park Bench, a restaurant they went to often. He got to the door of the restaurant first and could see written on a sheet of paper in large letters, 'Iranians Are Not Welcome.' He had flushed, turned around quickly and told Jennifer, "Let's go somewhere else." He remembered his most powerful emotion then had been more shame than anger. She had said, "No, we should protest, we should go in and eat there, they can't keep us out." "I don't want to," he had insisted. The whole evening had turned unpleasant, and he remembered how humiliated he had felt.

He discovered that feeling was common among all Iranians—many of the students and even older Iranians in town tried to hide where they came from. Once at the public library he asked the young man checking books if he was Iranian—because of his accent and a certain look about him. The boy blushed and after a moment of hesitation he stammered, "Yes, are you?" then quickly he turned away from Karim.

He had not even told Jennifer, and now could not bring himself to tell his uncle, about what happened to him on a late afternoon driving home on a quiet road through the woods outside of Athens. He had become aware of a car following him. The car swerved in front of his car and he had had to stop. He could see there were three men in it, gruff, angry looking men. The driver was holding a knife, waving it at him. Then the driver got out and came over to him, pointing the knife at his face. Karim remembered saying, "You have the wrong person, I don't know who you are." The man brought the knife closer: "But we know who you are." Luckily, a police car approached and his assailant must have seen it too, for he lowered the knife at once, got back into his car, and sped away.

Not long after that, he read something terrifying in the Athens newspaper: "Parviz Abadani, a fourteen-year-old Iranian boy, was beaten by his classmates and left in the empty lot behind Taft High School in Columbus. He was found by a man passing by, who had heard his moans. He was taken to the hospital and is in critical condition . . ." Karim had been so obsessed by the incident that he had gone to the empty lot and had stared for a long time at the ground, morbidly looking for signs of abuse. He had even tried to track down the boy's family but with no success.

It was as if a heavy weight had descended on him, pulling him down. He was startled sometimes when he saw his own reflection in a mirror. He had the tired, weary aura of someone who had been through an ordeal. His eyes had lost their luster. He looked ten years older than his age of thirty-six.

It's really incredible how vulnerable a human being can be, he thought. You are dealt enough blows and your sense of who you are, where you belong, crumbles.

"I started to detest the value system in America, the greed, the constant pressure and speed," Jamshid was saying. "People would pass by a dying man to make sure they would make it on time to their jobs." A dark cloud spread over his face. He pressed his cigarette into the wet saucer. "I shouldn't be smoking so much."

"You must quit altogether." Karim thought of his father who had died of an embolism in his brain, perhaps caused by smoking heavily. He had died suddenly, sitting at his desk at City Hall, where he was the chief clerk. Other employees had found him with his head resting on the desk. A flower, pinned that morning to the lapel of his jacket, lay next to his foot on the floor. After his father's death Jamshid had become a substitute father for him, giving him guidance and support.

"I quit, but then I started again, with all my ordeals . . ."

Karim was keenly aware of a frailty in his uncle, concealed so much of the time by his outgoing manner. It was an echo of the frailty he had seen this morning in Aziz's wrinkled face while she sat with him reminiscing. She had put her hand on his arm and kept it there, heavily, as if she needed to hang on to him with all the strength she had. "Remember, you used to say, 'Don't let me sleep later than five o'clock, I want to get up and do my schoolwork.' You wanted to be the best in your class and you were, always. Once you had fallen off your bicycle and a policeman brought you home. I was so frightened to see a policeman that I didn't notice your knees bleeding. Remember . . ."

He was surprised to find that she had kept in a box in the closet many of his belongings, records, books, notebooks, and letters he had written to her over the years. She had even saved a few of his kites. One was in the shape of a butterfly, yellow in color with stripes of black, another was the shape of a lantern and had a bright orange glow. The kites reminded him of the hours in early evening when he had stood on the roof flying them. He and other boys, with their kites, would call to each other, swing one kite against another as if in challenge. He had read some of his old letters. In nearly all the early ones he had expressed an almost missionary desire to return home and put his education to use there.

The waiter came over. "Do you want anything else?"

Jamshid looked at Karim. Karim shook his head. "I guess we should go back." Jamshid insisted on paying the bill, saying, "We're imposing on your mother. She wouldn't even let us pay her any rent." Anyway, Karim knew, it went against Jamshid's pride to let his nephew, younger than himself, pay.

The houses along the streets were in different styles—modern, old, poor, rich—and haphazardly set, some on elevated foundations. He looked into some of the rooms. A jade vase glowing in the afternoon sunlight, a photograph on a mantle, a pot of flowers on the windowsill. He tried to imagine living in one of those houses with Jennifer and Darius. It would be such a different life from Ohio.

It was amazing how alive the streets were in spite of the war damage, the weak economy—voices of shoppers, people going in and out of restaurants and houses, cars honking their horns, policemen blowing whistles, guiding traffic.

They passed a pottery shop. An old man with a long,

white beard and a withered face was sitting just inside the door. He seemed ancient, wise. It made Karim feel good to just look at that face. On the unpaved ground, not far from the pottery store, he spotted a blue tile partially covered with dirt. He picked it up and rubbed it with his hand. Fine particles of dust clung to his fingers. Then he put the tile in his pocket as if it were a talisman. At the beginning of the alley in which his mother's house stood, they stopped at the bakery to buy bread to take home.

"Three loaves," Karim told the man, who was baking bread on hot stones in an open oven.

"It will be only a moment," the man said, his dark, thin face red from the reflection of the fire as he slid thin slabs of dough from his wooden platen into the oven. At the end of his working day, Karim imagined, he would add up his receipts on an abacus with amber beads, put out the oven, and then go through the dark curtain in the back of the store, into his house where his wife and children awaited him.

In a few moments the man took out the baked loaves of bread with his platen and slid them onto the marble counter. Then with his fingers he removed the few pieces of gravel still stuck to them, folded the breads, and gave them to Karim. "God is still providing us with good flour. We should thank him for that."

In the alley several children were chasing each other, running and laughing, two others were throwing a ball back and forth in the air and catching it. Late afternoon sunlight cast a pink glow on everything. An image of his mother from long ago came to him. She was squatting by the door of the house, her chador tightly wrapped around her face, and staring down the street, waiting for his return.

"It took you all this time for one interview?" Jennifer, sitting with the other women in the courtyard, asked Karim as he and Jamshid came in.

"We had tea afterward," Karim said. Aware of an edge in Jennifer's voice he added quickly, "I'm sorry."

"Darius was very restless, I put him down in bed to get some rest," Jennifer said. "I'm worried about him."

"He's away from what he's used to." He handed the bread to his mother. "But he'll adjust, I'm sure."

"He's such a good boy, but of course traveling is hard on a child," Aziz said, putting the loaves in a basket under the tree and covering them with a thick piece of cloth.

Karim took off his jacket and hung it on a branch of the tree.

"No specific jobs yet," Jamshid said to Monir and their daughters. "But there are promises."

Karim noticed that Jennifer was avoiding conversation or eye contact with Jamshid. She had never liked him. When Jamshid had come to visit them in Ohio, she had told Karim, "I just can't take too much of him. You're different from him, cut from a different cloth, otherwise I couldn't live with you!" In some ways he couldn't blame her—Jamshid only addressed him when talking, and he always expected her to have food prepared for them. Still he wished she would be a little more tolerant, considering that he had to put up with boring, and sometimes infuriating, evenings at her parents' house. Once, when the Americans were still captive in Iran, her cousin, forgetting he was from Iran, had said, "We should round up all the Iranians in this country and put them in camps like we did with the Japanese."

He thought how once he had believed that love could conquer any obstacles. In those early days, when drunk with love for Jennifer, he would have laughed if anyone asked him, "Do the differences in your backgrounds ever create problems?" Anyway, falling in love was not a deliberate act. That was why it was called, "falling!" He could remember the precise moment he had fallen in love with Jennifer. It was as if he had no choice in the matter, as if he had been struck. He was looking at a photograph she had given him of herself when she was twelve years old. In the picture her hair was in pigtails and she was sitting on a swing holding onto the ropes. Something about the expression on her face, the color of her eyes, would not let go of him.

Before they began to live together he would call her sometimes just to hear her, the way she said hello in a quiet way, and how her voice gathered excitement as she said, "Karim, it's you." If she had a record on the phonograph, or was cooking something on the stove that she was afraid might burn, she would say, "Wait one minute." She would go away for a moment and come back and they would begin a long, leisurely conversation. Did she talk like that to other men? A sickening jealousy would come over him. It became an urgency to get to know her better, spend more time with her, have her in his bed every night if he could. She needed him too and no matter how often he wanted her, she responded. There was something so satisfying, no, magical, about that intense interlocking of their needs for each other. The air between them was always charged by a passionate energy. A mere glance at her creamy soft neck, her sparkling blond hair flowing over her shoulders as she stood by the bed in her nightgown instantly aroused a sexual response in him. When they moved in together he loved lying in bed and watching her get dressed. She would sing to herself as she combed her hair in front of the bureau mirror and put on her makeup. He would get up and put his arms around her and then slowly, sometimes to her playful protests, remove the clothes she had just put on, and take her back into bed again, not letting her go for a long time.

Karim paused in his reverie, interrupted by Darius, who had come out of his room, and was standing by the door in his pajamas.

"Oh, there you are, come over here, give your Daddy a kiss."

He climbed onto his lap. "Daddy, where did you go?"

"Looking for work for my uncle." He drew Darius close to him and hugged him.

"When are we going home? I want to play with Josh."

"Soon."

"You always say soon."

Karim laughed. How delightful Darius was with his tiny little defiances.

"He's a perfect combination of you and Jennifer," Monir said. "The curly blond hair hers, the brown eyes yours, the nose also yours."

"I have only one grandchild," Aziz said, picking up Darius from Karim's lap and putting him on her own. "Beautiful boy," she cooed, pushing her fingers through his hair. "Here, this is for you," She took out a red lollipop in the shape of a rooster from a large pocket in the front of her dress and put it in Darius's hand.

"Please, it isn't good for him to eat sweets," Jennifer protested.

Aziz stared at her with puzzled eyes.

Darius had begun to lick the lollipop. "I like this, Mom," he said.

It is going to be a losing battle, Karim thought. And no real harm will be done if he eats a few lollipops. A vendor shouted on the street, "We have live chicken for sale at low prices," and another cried, "We carry the best fruit and vegetables, we have eggs, the size you've never seen before."

Karim got up and went out to buy eggs. He remembered his father used to take out cash, which he always had loose in his pants' pockets, and give it to him. "Buy a dozen eggs," he used to say, or, "Get a tray of strawberries." The house then was filled with exquisite old rugs and furniture, chandeliers, china. His mother used to dress in pretty clothes and wear her hair long, almost to her waist. There were always people staying there—aunts, cousins, nieces, friends. In the month of Ramazan he would wake in the middle of the night to the voices of adults in the courtyard, talking and eating, breaking their day-long fasts. When he went out to join them, everyone would focus on him. "What a nice boy," "He is going to be more handsome even than his father." "He's so smart."

After her husband's death Aziz had changed almost irrevocably. She had begun to wear dark clothes, moved around slowly as if under a burden. She had developed sorrowful habits—the way she lowered her eyes and sighed. Habits that lingered over the years were now heightened by her recent tragedies.

He bought eggs from the old peddler.

"May God multiply your money by a hundred," the man said.

Karim came back inside and gave the eggs to his mother and she put them in the basket with the bread.

A muezzin's voice suddenly filled the air. "Allaho Akbar . . ."

Chapter 5

Jennifer waved to Karim as he left the room to join his uncle, who was waiting for him outside. The night before, he had told her that Jamshid had set up an interview in Naushahr, a town by the Caspian Sea, and suggested they all drive there. "You and Darius will get a chance to see the area. The seaside towns are very different from Teheran. For one thing they're lush and humid and the houses and buildings are painted in pastel colors," he had said. But she didn't think it was a good idea for Darius to be cooped up in the car. She told Karim he should go with his uncle and she'd stay home with Darius. Karim said he'd be back in a day or two.

She went into the courtyard and sat with the rest of the women, thinking painfully about the shadow spreading wider between her and Karim.

"Have more tea," Aziz said. The samovar, lit for breakfast, was still hissing. She began to pour tea into glasses from the kettle and to add water from the samovar.

Jennifer took one, so did Monir and the girls. Zohreh drank

hers while she read a novel, her attention riveted. Jennifer had noticed in Zohreh's room a bookcase full of books, many of them translations of American and European classics, but some by Iranian writers too, with whom Jennifer was actually familiar. One she knew was in exile in France after having been in jail a few times both under the shah and then under the new regime; another, a woman writer, had also been in jail under the new regime and was now hiding somewhere. Zohreh had told her she bought her books from a store that sold controversial titles under the counter. What amazed Jennifer was not so much the suffering and sadness expressed in those books, but that they had to be snuffed out. It made her anxious for Zohreh, who was so drawn to these voices, and whose own voice, whose own feelings of being oppressed, seemed to unite with theirs.

Azar was doing patchwork, sewing pieces of different fabrics together—a flying yellow bird next to a silk green leaf, a purple flower next to a red one. Azar had told her that she cut them out from clothes Aziz had saved from her youth and had given to her. It was a revelation to Jennifer that Aziz had once worn such colorful clothes. She wondered what she had been like then, when she was a young woman.

She had often wished her own mother and Aziz could meet. She saw certain similarities in the two women—they were both rigidly honest, both were religious, though they believed in different religions. They had devoted themselves to domesticity, though her mother had been a nurse once and had quit after she and her brother were born. Neither her mother or Aziz was a "modern" woman.

But of course there were great differences between them too. Aziz's big house was minimally furnished, although the heirloom rugs, the decoration around the fireplace, and the columns reminded her that it had once been different. The rooms now had only a few essentials—a rug, a bed, shelves built into the wall and hidden behind curtains to function as bureaus. Only Zohreh's and Azar's shared room had some special, personal decorations—a shortwave radio on which they somehow got American music, a phonograph, some records, and Zohreh's books. On the wall over Zohreh's bed were photographs of American actresses—Elizabeth Taylor, Marilyn Monroe, Meryl Streep, and many others—that she must have cut from magazines, old ones, because in new publications they did not allow such pictures, or if they did, the women's faces were blotted out by dark ink, something Jennifer found terrifying to look at. Over Azar's bed was a poster of a popular Iranian singer.

Jennifer's mother's house was the opposite of Aziz's in that it was cluttered with years of shopping, full of things she had bought, whether she needed them or not, at flea markets, garage sales, at the auctions she went to sometimes on Saturday nights. Flowery plates, an antique commode, all sorts of colored glasses. Every room had more furniture than it needed. Windowsills were covered by decorative glass items that glinted in the sun. The kitchen shelves were full to the brim with dishes and glasses, including her mother's set of chartreuse glass dishes (called Vaseline glass), mugs, goblets, salt and pepper shakers, candleholders, plates, and bowls.

She thought that all in all her mother would enjoy Aziz—oddly, in spite of her rigidities, she'd always had an openness, even more, a yearning to learn about other worlds. When Jennifer was a child her mother had given her a collection of foreign dolls for her birthday—one Romanian, one Swedish, one Indian. Her mother liked the idea that an Indian family was running the supermarket nearby, that a Hungarian woman had opened up a restaurant. "Foreigners bring color," she said. She had said something about Karim that had affected Jennifer deeply, "He has the kindest, warmest eyes of anyone I know." (Her father's reaction to Karim was ambiguous, harder to read—he often made remarks that revealed his ignorance of a larger world.)

Darius came out of the room and joined them. "How do you feel?" his grandmother asked.

Darius just rubbed his eyes.

"I have something for you," Aziz said. She went into her room and came back holding a box. She gave it to Darius.

Darius opened it. Inside lay a gold pendant with the word, "Allah," engraved on it.

Looking deep into Darius's eyes, Aziz said, "Let the spirit of God enter you while you're a child. God is always watching you, what you do now on this earth. Your actions on this earth will determine whether you will go to heaven or hell."

Darius nodded, awe-struck, it seemed, though he could not have understood every word.

Yesterday Jennifer had seen him kneeling with his grandmother with *mohrs* set on prayer rugs spread before them, Aziz saying the prayers aloud and Darius repeating after her, as they bowed down, putting their foreheads on the *mohrs* for a moment, and then rising.

I hope she's not going to try to make me pray, Jennifer thought uneasily. She remembered her battles with her own mother about religion—her refusal to go to church, when she was an adolescent, had been a source of tension between them. Aziz had already said to her, "Hundreds of men were martyred for a holy cause. If I could put some religious feelings into you while you're in my house . . ." Aziz had given her two chadors, a black one for outside and a white one with floral designs to wear around the house in the presence of male guests. Otherwise a scarf, a *roopush* (a raincoat-like garment), and dark stockings would have been sufficient as far as the law was concerned.

Aziz took the pendant from Darius's hand and put it around his neck. "Now God will be with you all the time."

Her religion seemed to guide her every action. "It's up to God, if I live for another day." "If God wills it." She used these phrases very frequently.

She had been trying to get Karim to pray. Karim had done so once in a while, clearly just to please her. Not that everyone in the household prayed. As far as Jennifer could see only Aziz and Monir did and Monir clearly to accommodate Aziz.

On their first visit religion had not been much of an issue, maybe because she and Karim were here only for two weeks. At that time, the main thing that had concerned Aziz was whether they had a Moslem wedding ceremony, and Karim had reassured her in this.

"Mommy, I want to go to heaven," Darius said to Jennifer suddenly in English. "I'll have lots of candies and cakes to eat there and toys to play with. There's only fire in hell."

Jennifer smiled but did not bother translating what he said for Aziz. It would only encourage her.

"These are the most comfortable shoes I've ever had," Aziz said to her, pointing to the clumpy black shoes made of soft leather she had taken off and put next to the rug. Jennifer had bought them, at Aziz's own request, along with other presents. Aziz had described what she wanted in such detail that Jennifer had spotted them right away in the window of a Florsheim shoe store in a Columbus mall. "I'm an old woman, my legs ache all the time."

It always startled Jennifer that Aziz referred to herself as old. She was fifty-seven, only a year older than her own mother, who never saw herself that way.

Sinking into a melancholy mood, Aziz added, "Karim used to tell me he would come home after he finished his education. This is only the second time he's been back."

Jennifer could feel the weight of the blame. "We'll be coming back more often now that it's become easier. And of course we'd be happy if you came to America."

"If I come to America, where will America go?"

Jennifer could understand how Aziz felt. She remembered meeting an Iranian woman Aziz's age with the same strong adherence to Islam who lived with her son in Columbus. The woman had been sitting cross-legged in a corner in her son's house during a party and complaining to whomever was willing to listen, "Why doesn't my son take me back home, what's here for me?" Tears had fallen from her eyes. Her son had told Jennifer that the old woman insisted on washing her own clothes by hand and hanging them to dry out in the sun so that they wouldn't be washed with his non-Moslem wife's clothes in the washing machine. She asked him to read the ingredients on every food package to make sure no pork or pork fat was used in it because it was against Moslem dietary laws. He had to have meat or poultry slaughtered in the correct Moslem way for her. He had to buy a pitcher for her to use in the bathroom instead of toilet paper.

Monir took out a white pill from a jar next to the samovar and swallowed it with a few gulps of her tea. "Take one," she said to Aziz. "It soothes the nerves." She took several kinds of pills every day—multivitamins, iron, and calcium. This one seemed to be a tranquilizer. She offered them freely to whoever was willing to take them.

Aziz took the pill, with her tea also. "I was lonely before you came to live with me," she said to Monir. "Now you're all here and Karim is back too. What will I do if you go away again? Do you know what it was like for me without you? Day after day alone in this house, sometimes with only the birds and the fish, and the alley cat to keep me company."

There was a knock on the outside door, then the sound of footsteps approaching. A young man, holding a large bouquet of flowers, came into the courtyard.

"Oh, Hossein, how nice of you to come," Aziz said. "Sit down, have some tea." The samovar was still hissing.

"Please don't go to any trouble. I have only a few moments. I have to be back at my shop but I wanted to visit for a little while."

"It's no trouble, sit down."

He gave the bouquet to Aziz and she walked away with it.

She came back momentarily with a vase holding the flowers and put it in the middle of the cloth, then she poured tea for the visitor.

He put several pieces of rock sugar in his tea, practically filling up half of the glass, and kept stirring it, then he drank it in a few gulps as if his body were deprived of sweetness. His hands, fat and dimpled, gave the same impression of gentleness as his round face did. "Your tea is always excellent, a beautiful amber color, and just the right fragrance." Turning to Jennifer he said, "Welcome. I hope you don't find our country too difficult right now. I've been meaning to come over ever since I heard you and Karim were visiting. I was sorry I didn't come to the airport to meet you."

"Thank you, you're very kind," Jennifer said, cheered up by the young man's gay spirits.

"How long are you staying?" he asked.

"Two months altogether."

"You've come a long way, why go back so soon?"

"Darius has school and Karim and I have our work."

"There's always work to do, it will get done eventually."

While he was talking to Jennifer, his eyes often returned to Zohreh.

When he finished his tea, he got up. "I'd better go."

"Won't you stay for lunch?" Aziz asked.

"I'll come back again for a longer visit." He said goodbye, his eyes lingering on Zohreh. Zohreh's face became intense with emotion. He glanced at Aziz and Monir, who were engaged in a conversation and then reached over and surreptitiously squeezed Zohreh's arm. She did not respond to his touch, Jennifer noticed.

He started for the door, swaying as he walked. His manner was a combination of gentleness and masculinity.

As soon as he was out of the door Aziz said, "He's a second cousin, related to us by marriage. He's such a nice young man, he'd make a fine husband for Zohreh."

"Please," Zohreh said, blushing. She and her sister got up and went back into their room.

"My daughters are very particular," Monir said to Jennifer, a furrow of sadness appearing between her eyebrows. "They had so many suitors when we had our own home." As if Jennifer could not judge for herself, Monir explained, "Azar is prettier in the conventional sense. She's always had a perfect complexion and her curls are natural. Zohreh has more magnetism."

"They both are attractive, accomplished young women," Jennifer said.

There was another knock on the door and other visitors began to stream in.

Chapter 6

Karim and Jamshid took turns driving the old Mercedes, one luxury Jamshid had kept from his employed days. They went more slowly when they reached the towns along the Caspian Sea. Miles of rice fields stretched between the towns. A few times Karim had asked Jamshid to stop so that he could take photographs—of a mosque with blue minarets, a steep stairway leading down to a spring, the steps crowded with people carrying jugs to fill with water, a field being irrigated by horse-drawn equipment, an intricate maze of alleys.

Jamshid began to smoke a cigarette, taking long drags and inhaling deeply. Then, abruptly, he put out the cigarette. "It's suicidal for me to be smoking, with my bad heart."

"You never said anything to me about a bad heart."

"It isn't that serious, it's just that my doctor told me to be careful."

"Jamshid, this should be the last cigarette you smoke."

"I know. I'll quit as soon as I start working; that's my latest resolution."

They passed through an ancient village full of historical sights—a *karvansary*, a castle. They made their way through an alley so narrow that the walls seemed to be closing in above them, forming a tunnel.

Jamshid patted his arm. "You're preoccupied, is it still that letter?"

"So many problems are waiting for me."

"You do have alternatives, you know."

They had reached Naushahr. The town was surrounded on three sides by jagged mountains, on the fourth by the sea. Its streets were lined with immense fir trees. Elegant, whitewashed villas stood side by side with burnt-out buildings, destroyed by bombs and not rebuilt yet. There was more war damage visible here than in Teheran. They passed a dilapidated house, where a family, a woman and a man and two children, were sleeping all together under a huge beige army blanket in one of the rooms. The children kept twisting around as if in pain. Outside the house stood a glass case displaying an enlarged photograph of a young man. Underneath it was written, "Martyr Farhang Naghdi, Died in the Holy War." He had a handsome, innocent face, large, dark eyes, high forehead, full lips and a thin mustache. Guilt gripped Karim's heart. How devastating it must have been to be bombed, to lose your children and others close to you. In a park in the middle of town, rows of men were sitting on benches, most of them with crutches at their sides. War veterans, no doubt. He had read that there was a high concentration of them in these seaside towns, where they now tried to make a living by fishing.

"A lot of these veterans are addicted," Jamshid said. "They steal caviar from the state packaging plant here and exchange it for drugs. They also get vodka from the Russian sailors that way." He parked his car in front of the Arise Construction Company and they got out. The street was crowded with people coming in and out of offices and shops, vendors displaying crafts out in the open—handmade pottery and jewelry, wooden boxes. Men dealing in the black market lurked in doorways, exchanging foreign money or selling rare items. Everything, even liquor and American videos, seemed to be available in the huge black market.

Karim followed his uncle into the building and they looked for the office where the interview was to be held, then he waited in the reception room while his uncle went in. On the sofa across from him several other people were waiting. One of them, a middle-aged woman, was poring over some documents.

Before long Jamshid returned with another man whom he introduced to Karim as "Khosro Ghotbi."

Karim got up and they shook hands.

"I'd like to talk to you in my office for a few moments, if I could," Khosro said.

Khosro sat behind his desk and Karim sat across from him. The room was pleasant, with pale blue walls and oak furniture.

"Your uncle was telling me about you. With your education in urban planning you would be very valuable here in Iran. Would you consider working for us, at one of our branches, here or in Teheran? So many of our educated people have left the country just when they're needed the most." He had an easy, self-confident manner.

"Thank you but I really can't take a job here. I'll be returning to the United States at the end of the summer."

"We have several projects going already, restoring mosques and historical sites that were damaged by bombs, planning parks," Khosro persisted. "We'll provide you and your family with subsidized housing, and give you a Paykan car. The starting salary is competitive."

"It's tempting but really not possible for me."

"The position is available immediately this fall," Khosro went on. "All you need to do is to provide me with your vita."

The two of them talked for a while. Khosro himself had been educated in England. "You know, my life has more meaning here. I had a good life there, but I knew I'd never be really and truly an Englishman. I'm an Iranian. And I'm more needed here than anywhere else."

Karim smiled and got up, feeling his heartbeat accelerate. This man would hire him right then and there.

Khosro saw him to the door and they shook hands again.

Jamshid was pacing around the waiting room. He stopped as soon as he saw Karim. "Don't dismiss the idea," he said to him.

"What happened with your own interview?" Karim asked.

"It's promising. Frankly, he was more interested in you than in me. Do you want to spend the night in Naushahr?"

"We may as well, it's getting late."

"I know of a good hotel. I stayed there once."

They got into the car and drove along the green, thickly wooded coast to the hotel.

The hotel was small but clean and inviting, faced with stucco and brick, surrounded by fruit trees and flowering shrubs. Jamshid asked the clerk for a room with two beds.

"We have one available on the second floor."

Karim followed his uncle up the stairs. In the corridor a maid was folding sheets and putting them in a closet. The doors were all painted bright yellow. Their room overlooked the sea and was colorfully furnished with a purple, blue, and yellow kilim on the floor and yellow bedspreads. Karim looked out of the window at children playing on the beach; one threw a ball and ran after it while others were holding strings of kites that fluttered high in the sky. "I should call Jennifer, I want to know how Darius is doing," he said to Jamshid who was washing up in the bathroom. He went to the phone and asked the operator to dial Aziz's number. After a few rings someone picked up.

"Hello." It was Jennifer herself.

"Jennifer . . . we're in Naushahr."

Silence, filled with tension, followed.

"Jamshid just had the interview. How's Darius, can I talk to him?"

"He went to bed."

She sounded remote. "He doesn't have temperature or diarrhea, does he?" he asked.

"No, he's just tired all the time."

"Well, if he doesn't have . . ."

Suddenly the phone seemed to have gone dead. He couldn't hear anything. "Hello, hello, hello," he said, then hung up. At least he had managed to say the essential things, he thought. He sat there holding his head in his hands.

"Are you all right?" Jamshid asked.

"I couldn't really talk to her. The line went dead."

Chapter 7

Before they entered the hotel restaurant, the clerk approached Karim and his uncle and said, "If you need anything let me know." He added in a near whisper, "Everything is available at reasonable prices. You could have a *sigheh* for one night, two nights, whatever you like. An *aghound* is on the premises to perform the ceremony."

Karim shook his head, feeling uneasy.

"I promise we have the best—we give them tests to make sure they have no diseases."

"We'll let you know," Jamshid said.

The restaurant was attractive. There were pink tablecloths and pink-shaded lamps hanging on the walls, and candles set on tables. A few families and a couple of single men, probably on business, were eating at scattered tables. Liquor was being served freely, the local police having been paid off perhaps. They ordered wine along with food.

Jamshid picked up his glass, "Let's toast to your homecoming."

Karim raised his glass and touched it to Jamshid's. Two women wrapped in *chadors* came and stood before them.

"Can we be of any help?" one of them, younger-looking than the other, asked Karim. "You know . . ." Then the two of them sat down across the table from them, not waiting for an invitation.

"We're just passing through," Karim said awkwardly.

The other woman and Jamshid were already engaged in conversation. He heard her say to Jamshid, "Let him know, if you want to." She was pointing to the clerk who was now talking to the cashier.

Jamshid leaned over Karim and whispered, "Do you want to?"

"I don't see how . . ." Karim whispered back.

"It's legitimate, if they perform that ceremony, I mean as far as the law is concerned. We won't get into trouble."

"I know, but . . ." The younger woman had a gentle, sensitive manner, the other woman was more wary, her brown eyes expressing a hardness. Still, they both could easily pass as their wives.

The lights had gone off and now the place was lit only by candles, creating a romantic atmosphere.

The younger woman reminded him of someone . . . it was what-was-her-name, Jhaleh, a young girl he had had a crush on when he was an adolescent. It was an understanding of things beyond their years that they both projected. Jhaleh used to live in the house across the street. He would go to the roof and stand there waiting for her to come out, just to catch a glimpse of her. Sometimes she came to the porch of her house, her dark, wavy hair hanging loose over her shoulders, and leaned against a column or wrapped her arms around it. Eye contact was as far as their flirtation went, but it was enough to bring him back to the roof the next day. He had finally written a letter, asking her to meet him at a cinema in a distant neighborhood, where no one would recognize them. He had slipped the letter into her hand as he passed her on the street. She came as he had asked. They met secretly a few times. Before he left the country he had told her, "I'll be back after college and we'll get married." What had happened to her, where was she? Aziz had told him that their house was sold to another family years ago. His life would have been so entirely different if he had married her, simpler maybe . . .

The two women got up. "You can reach us through him," the older woman said, pointing to the clerk. Then the two of them walked away.

Karim and Jamshid lingered a while longer.

"I'm amazed this kind of thing is still available, even underground," Karim said.

"You can't take away what people are used to. But most of what they fought for in the revolution—more equality of wealth among the people, less corruption and brutality by the government—has been achieved."

"Did you back the revolution?"

"I had mixed feelings about it as I watched it happening."

"I don't like the intolerance toward other religions," Karim said.

"I know what you mean. Most of our Bahais and Jews, for instance, among the most educated, have fled, fearing persecutions," Jamshid said. "Remember my friend Roofeh, he helped you with your passport and visa, he always asked about you. He and his family left for Israel right after the revolution." He went on, "But you know I had lost respect for the shah. He was trying too hard to imitate the West. At the Shiraz celebration, they served French food, and put on plays and movies by American directors. Where was Iranian culture?"

Karim had always been aware of this ambivalence in his uncle. After he had finished his one year training in Texas he was offered a very good job in Dallas. He could have stayed on—his wife and children would have been happy to join him—but he had chosen to return home even though the country was still under the shah's rule.

"And you know how terrifying the *savak* was. It was so much larger and more systematic than the *pasdars* now," Jamshid added.

They talked and drank a little more, then they went back to their room.

"Do you want to see Babolsar before we go back to Teheran?" Jamshid asked Karim after breakfast. "Then we could stop and see my sister too."

"Sure. It's been so many years since I saw Aunt Khadijeh." He remembered how much he used to like to visit his aunt. As a child his mother took him there and when he was a little older he went there in the summer and sometimes stayed for weeks. It would be nice to visit her and at the same time take notes on the town's plan as he had at Naushahr earlier that morning.

As soon as they checked out of the hotel, they headed toward Naushahr. In a short while, the old Mercedes began to steam up, the temperature gauge going way up.

"This is a very old car, I need to get a new one once I have a job," Jamshid said. He opened the hood and they looked in. Water was dripping from the radiator and the ground under the front wheels was wet. "We should take it to a gas station. Luckily we didn't go too far." They got back into the car and Jamshid began to drive back to Naushahr, slowly. They spotted a gas station on a wide main street and stopped.

A young man was standing at the pumps, wearing khaki overalls stained with oil. "My radiator seems to have a leak," Jamshid said to him.

"Let me look at it."

Karim and Jamshid stood by as the man examined it.

"Yes, it's broken."

"Can you fix it today?" Jamshid asked.

The man shook his head. "It won't be ready until tomorrow afternoon, more likely the next day."

Jamshid took their bags out of the trunk and gave the car keys to the attendant. "We'll have to go back to the hotel," he said to Karim as they walked away. After they checked in, Karim tried to call Jennifer, but this time the line was busy. He finally gave up and he and Jamshid went for a walk. They found a shop on the main square and Karim bought a pair of earrings made of crystal chandelier drops for Jennifer, a leather belt for Darius, and a silk scarf for Aziz. Jamshid bought some presents too. They resumed walking, passing a cluster of white stucco buildings with low domes, mud and straw houses, huts. In one spot two old women were sitting on a porch, knitting a rug. Everything about the sights and sounds of Iran penetrated Karim deeply as if hollows had been carved inside him during the years of his absence and were now being filled.

It was getting hot as noon approached. "Why don't we go to the beach behind the hotel. We can get something to eat there," Jamshid suggested.

They went through the park, walking in the shade of fir trees. Jamshid was suddenly quiet. Then he stopped and leaned against a tree. Karim was startled to see tears streaming down his face.

"Uncle, what's wrong, cars break down once in a while." How strange it was to see Jamshid, who had always been strong and optimistic, cry. He used to make Karim laugh, to give a glitter and magic to everything when they went for walks together.

"It isn't the car, it's what my life has come to," Jamshid said through tears. "I still have nightmares about bombs being dropped on our heads. I saw terrible things happen to people—a man abandoned on the side of the road with one of his hands severed, another man with his skull split, a beggar woman with her baby in her arms, both of them dead. When a missile hit our house, for an instant I thought the explosion was thunder. Then—it was unbelievable—a part of my house had disappeared. I ran frantically everywhere, trying to find the others. Monir and my daughters were crying for days."

"I wish I'd been there to help you."

"Never mind. You're here now. This trip, being with you, means so much to me."

Karim took out a piece of tissue from his shirt pocket and gave it to his uncle. Jamshid wiped his tears.

"It must have been an extraordinary feeling to have peace finally," Karim said. "I know how good I felt when I glanced at the headlines early one morning and saw it had happened. I called my Iranian friends to tell them the news in case they hadn't heard. We went out and celebrated together that night."

"For us it was different," Jamshid said. "We were still deep in the wreckage."

Chapter 8

Karim was reading a local newspaper as he waited on the hotel beach for his uncle, who had gone inside to buy a pack of cigarettes, obviously unable to cut down. "The new mayor of Teheran is planning to put two hundred parks in place of some of the buildings destroyed by war . . ." His thoughts drifted to Jennifer, the implicit assumption on her part that he would be the one who had to live in a foreign country for the rest of his life.

The issue had come up on different occasions. Though he had never really stated a desire to return to Iran permanently, Jennifer seemed afraid of it. For instance their argument after that terrible dinner party Nancy and Don had arranged. The Porters and the Elliotts were there too—they lived in the neighborhood and the men were affiliated with an engineering consulting company. Jennifer said something about their going to Iran for a visit. "I wouldn't go there for anything," Jack Porter said, his watery pale green eyes flickering with something like indignation. "They kept our men there for four hundred and forty-three days, it's incredible they let them out alive."

"But they *did* let them out alive," Karim said, feeling his heart beating painfully. His voice came out breathless.

"Karim and I want to see his family, it will be good for Darius too," Jennifer said.

Jack only shook his head faintly.

On their way home in the car Karim said, "I can't stand any of these people, they're so ignorant and narrow-minded. I wish we could get away from this place altogether." Jennifer, assuming he had Iran in mind, had said, "But this is our home. The house is finally in good shape, Darius has his friends here. And we both have our work. You know how much I love my job."

He saw the shadow of someone approaching, it was a woman, who came and sat in front of him. "Do you remember me?"

"Of course." He recognized the prostitute immediately—the large, shy eyes, the sensual lips. She was so young.

"Your friend sent me here. He's talking to my friend inside." He could smell her musky perfume. "I thought you were going to be here only one night."

"Our car broke down, so we're staying a little longer."

"I left my village, my nine brothers and sisters, and came here to earn a living. Now I can send them some money," she said as if appealing to his mercy. "I miss my little brother the most, he's ten years old."

She is just a child herself, he thought.

"You can have me as a *sigheh* tonight," she said, her tone wavering between pleading and flirtation, her eyes staring into his, moving him.

He felt a quickening in his blood. When was the last time I spent a night with a woman other than Jennifer, he thought? More than a decade. Jennifer was the only American woman I took seriously.

"Your friend wants you to."

"He's my uncle."

"Oh, your uncle."

Can I really go ahead with this ridiculous idea, marrying this stranger for one night? I could give her some money and let her go. She was looking at him, waiting. Her eyes, so much like Jhaleh's; and she was wearing the same musky perfume Jhaleh used to wear. So many unfulfilled promises.

He took out his wallet and gave her some *toomans*. She looked at it and her face beamed.

"My name is Soroor, in case you want to find me," she said, getting up.

Karim watched her walk away, a prostitute, wrapped in a chador, walking on the beach. How absurd. But then he had the sensation that he had lost something by letting her go.

In a moment Jamshid came back. "We could go through the ritual and then have their company all night," he said. "We've seen all there is to see in town."

Karim stared down at the sand. "I don't know, the whole thing is strange . . ."

"It's better for the prostitutes this way, they're better protected. Some of these women are intelligent, have something to say."

Jennifer, Karim thought, but he was unable to push down the aching yearning the prostitute had awakened in him.

Early in the evening he, Jamshid, and the two women gathered in the hotel room and an *aghound* arrived almost immediately after. He had a lively manner and he looked striking with his long beard and nails painted red with henna. The two women were now wearing light-colored chadors, one with floral designs and the other with geometrical shapes. They all sat on chairs around the room and the *aghound* read a sermon from the Koran he had brought with him, marrying Karim to the younger woman and Jamshid to the other, for one night. It was very simple—he read the sermon and asked each person if he or she agreed to the temporary marriage. Then he set the price the men would pay for the night.

It is so incredible for me to be doing this, Karim thought.

The porter came in, carrying a tray with a teapot, cups, and sugar on it. He put the tray on the table and left promptly.

After they had tea, the *aghound* got up. Smiling, he said, "Now you have God's blessing."

Karim and Jamshid paid him. As soon as he was out of the door the women pushed off their chadors, letting them slip over their shoulders. They were both wearing light makeup and their clothes were of subdued colors.

"We're nice girls," Mina, the older girl, said, catching Karim's eyes.

"Mina, don't bore them," Soroor said.

"I had my palm read once by a gypsy," Mina went on. "She told me I was going to get married soon and have eight children." She giggled.

"Shall we take a walk into town and have dinner there?" Jamshid suggested.

"That's a good idea," Karim said.

Chapter 9

Karim, Jamshid, and the prostitutes left the hotel and began to walk toward the square which was bright with lanterns hanging on shop doors. Jewelry and glass ornaments glittered in the shop windows. In one corner a man was putting silver paint on a colander. He dipped the colander into a pot of silvery liquid and then held it with a fork high over a fire burning in a stove to solidify the coating. A group of dervishes in white robes were dancing in the middle of the square, pulling some of the passersby into their circle.

The spark of desire was growing in Karim in anticipation of spending the night with Soroor, though it had been arbitrary that she had put herself with him, probably because she was a little younger, and Mina had gone with Jamshid.

"There's a good restaurant down that road. It's really a rooming house, but they let you eat there as well," Mina said. "It's inside a garden, secluded."

"Let's go there then," Jamshid said.

They went through a gate into the garden and walked

down a path lined by lush, thick bushes and trees, redolent with fruit. Light bulbs, strung through the branches, lit the way for them.

A man, wearing baggy pants and a loose shirt with the sleeves rolled up, was standing on a raised platform under the trees. He stared down at them and then his face lit up. "You have brought guests for me," he said to Mina.

They went up onto the platform and sat on the carpet-covered floor, leaning against pillows. The man and a ruddy-faced woman, who seemed to be his wife, went in and out of a room, bringing back food—mutton marinated in spices, rice mixed with lima beans and dill, salad. "We grow everything here and we have our own sheep," the man said.

The aroma of food was mixed with the fragrance of early evening flowers.

An orange, long-haired cat came over and curled up on Soroor's lap. She kept stroking its back as it purred. A woman's voice on the radio flowed out of a room, singing. "Oh night, come faster, come and fold me into your layers of darkness, for I want to get lost, get lost in you . . . come faster . . ."

Jamshid had lit a cigarette and he was inhaling it deeply and then blowing out the smoke hard into the air, away from everyone.

"You haven't really slowed down, uncle," Karim said.

Jamshid put the cigarette out, pushing it to the edge of his plate. He turned to the owner who was standing in the doorway of the room. "Can we have vodka or wine?"

"I have both."

"Bring some of each."

The man went inside and came back with bottles of wine and vodka for them. "Two rooms are ready for you, if you want to stay the night," he said and walked away. Soroor and Mina got up and went inside too, to use the bathroom it seemed.

"Places like this mainly charge for the food, they add very little for the rooms," Jamshid said.

"We may as well stay then."

Jamshid filled their glasses and they began to drink. The sky was covered with bright stars and a moon that looked like it had been cut exactly in half. Fireflies sparkled between tree branches.

The two women came back. Soroor reached over and touched Karim's hair, "You have such nice hair," she said. He took her hand and held it for a moment. She put her arm around his waist and he could feel the warmth of her body against his. He tried to talk to her. "How long have you lived in Naushahr? Did you finish high school?"

Jamshid ordered more drinks. Karim indulged in glass after glass of wine. It was past midnight when they all got up and went into the rooms the owner had gotten ready for them.

Karim lay on the bed with all his clothes on. I am going to pass out. The thought went through his mind fleetingly. I have never been so drunk in my life. He tried to focus on various things in the room, a bureau, a chair, a rug. The print curtains on the window and a lamp with a burgundy glass shade gave out a warm glow that created a homey, cozy atmosphere.

He felt Soroor's hands on his body. She was undressing him.

Then he felt her beside him on the bed, her naked skin. He smelled the musky perfume again.

Everything around him was blurry. He moved his hand along her body tentatively. A memory flashed across his hazy mind. He was walking at the edge of a ravine somewhere in the countryside—he must have been about thirteen or fourteen—and heard a shrill cry down below. He was shocked to see a woman running in the ravine, her blouse torn, one of her breasts exposed, and a man chasing her. Blood was flowing from the scratches on her bare breast, chest, arm. A few days later he heard a prostitute had been stoned to death, not far from that spot. He had wondered if it had been that woman. One day I will have some influence in changing such horrors, he had thought in his adolescent idealism.

He had to fight a wave of nausea rising in him. He felt Soroor's hand moving on his chest, stomach. Am I going to manage . . .

He saw a naked woman walking toward a room. The word "Toilet" on a plaque nailed to the door caught his eye. Tree branches were thrashing against each other in the wind outside. As she walked out of the bathroom a ray of light coming through the curtains outlined her body. A narrow waist, pear-shaped breasts, slender long legs. A sharp pang of desire shot up in him. "Soroor," he called.

She came and lay next to him. They turned to each other and he kissed her, feeling himself getting hard. Her dark hair spread on the white pillow, her breasts flattened against her rib cage. He kissed one breast and then the other. He kissed her navel, thighs. He moved into her easily . . .

At dawn she got out of the bed and began to put her clothes on. He sat up and reached for his pants on the chair. He took his wallet from the pocket and gave 10,000 *toomans* to her, twice as much as they had agreed to. She tossed the money into her purse without comment, put her *chador* on, and kissed him on the cheek.

"Do you want to stay?" Karim asked.

Soroor shook her head. "My friend has to go somewhere." She smiled sweetly. "I'll find you at the beach by your hotel." She said goodbye casually and left as if this were not the end between them.

He lay back on the bed. Was another man waiting for her in another room? Would she act the same with the other man? There was a sincere quality in her, had that been a mere act? What about diseases? The hotel clerk had said, "We give them tests." The chances are it was true. He felt a stab of guilt, thinking how much Jennifer would detest this if she knew about it. But in a way, he thought, sleeping with this prostitute, for one night, in a drunken state, was nothing. It was merely embracing a memory, bringing back through touch someone else from another stage of his life.

A soft knock sounded on the door and Jamshid came in. "Are you ready?"

"I will be in a minute," Karim said, not looking at him, suddenly shy.

Jamshid won't give it much thought or try to analyze the meaning or consequences of what we did, now that it happened, he thought. In a way he wished he could be lighthearted about it himself. But then as he glanced at Jamshid, he detected a little sadness, a vague hint of something—regret maybe, shame.

"Who knows if we'll be alive tomorrow," Jamshid mumbled.

Chapter 10

A ray of sunlight glared down on Jennifer. She was sweaty and her head ached. There was a bitter taste in her mouth. She must have fallen asleep. Then she remembered that Darius was still not himself and that Karim had left her with the responsibility and was still off somewhere with his uncle. She saw, through the open door, that Aziz now was sitting with Darius in the courtyard, reading to him:

> All save the face of
> God doth perish.
> To him shall we return.
> God is all-pervading, All-knowing.
> Praise be to Allah, Lord of the Worlds,
> Show us the straight path . . .

She wondered what Karim felt about his mother indoctrinating Darius. Over the years they had had many discussions about what kind of religious training, if any, they should provide for Darius. Maybe a Unitarian church would be good, maybe something of each religion, Moslem and Christian. They had ended up giving him no training. And then they had decided to send him to Juniper Tree School because the majority of the children attending it came from mixed religious and cultural backgrounds. They had met some of the mothers. When they heard someone addressing Mrs. Furumoto, a blond American responded, and Mrs. O'Conner was Chinese . . .

She lay there, distraught, wondering how she was going to bear the rest of this visit. They had been there for three weeks now, but it seemed like an eternity.

The ceiling fan had stopped turning because of an electrical failure, which seemed to happen two, three times a day, and it was stiflingly hot in the room. She felt nostalgic for the mist in the air over the fields where she went on walks near their house in Athens, the cool breeze that always blew when they sat on the patio. She was even nostalgic for her daily routine at home—exercise, dropping off Darius at his nursery school, and then going to work—she worked three days in the Columbus office and two days at home. On the days that she worked in the city Karim picked up Darius, since he had no afternoon courses to teach, and stayed with him until she returned from work. She liked to make lists for herself with headings, "Call Nancy at nine," "Take Darius to his swimming lesson at six," and then check off each item as she got it done.

Now she had to try to fit in with Karim's family's rituals—tea, snacks, long lunches, afternoon naps, prayers. Every morning Aziz watered and weeded the plants, swept the ground, made sure the kerosene lamps had enough oil—they had to have the lamps ready for when the electricity went out. Monir got the day started with her own and some of her two daughters' personal chores, washing, ironing, sewing. She and her daughters always dressed in fresh, nice clothes. Monir wore linen skirts and blouses and sandals, and large gold jewelry. Azar liked full, printed skirts and frilly blouses, and delicate filigree gold jewelry. Zohreh almost always wore jeans and T-shirts and a thin chain necklace. (Of course they all wore chadors over their clothes when they went out and Aziz wore a chador even when they had male visitors at home.)

Aziz rarely left the house. Occasionally Monir went out shopping with her daughters or visited a relative or friend. But she too stayed home most of the time. Zohreh was the only one who used every opportunity to go out. She even took on all the grocery shopping so that she could get away from the house.

Azar had once wanted to be a stewardess so that she could fly all over the world and still always come back home, but after the revolution it had become more difficult for a woman to hold a job like that. Now she spent her time embroidering, or playing cards with whomever would play with her, or she hung around with her friend, Latifeh, a young girl her own age who lived in the house next door. If Zohreh was away, Latifeh and Azar went into their bedroom and sang together, songs about loneliness and unrequited love, or they listened to records with the same themes. Or they danced, snapping their fingers as they gyrated their hips. Sometimes Latifeh would suddenly stop whatever she was doing as if she had heard an emergency bell and say, "I have to go, my mother is alone," her voice expressing urgency. Her mother was paralyzed from the waist down, due to a inept operation, Latifeh explained, so she had all the responsibility of caring for her since she was the only child and her father had died long ago.

Zohreh told Jennifer that before her father had lost his job, he had promised to send her abroad for an education. Now she hoped to get into Teheran University which was almost free and she could also save money living at home. Her parents expected to look for a place of their own as soon as Jamshid found work, she said. In the fall Azar planned to go to the local high school to finish her last year, which had been interrupted, but her goals beyond high school were not clear yet. Zohreh wanted to study comparative literature and in the fall she would be taking English and Italian at the university until she could apply to become fully matriculated.

Most days Karim and Jamshid went to the stone basement to lift weights, but the women in the household did nothing for exercise. Accustomed to taking vigorous long walks and bicycling, Jennifer felt her muscles becoming slack, and a restlessness in her body for more movement. She had begun to do some running in place and some sit-ups but that did not entirely satisfy her. It was hard for Darius, too. Karim had found a tricycle for him, which he had gotten cheap at a used bicycle shop in Teheran. At first Darius rode around and around the courtyard on it, then he gave it up—partly because it became monotonous and partly because he just wasn't feeling well.

Every day there were many visitors, friends, and relatives—a tall young woman who complained of backaches due to lifting up the children too much, a round-faced pretty woman who smiled a lot, revealing her dimples, a woman who had twin girls. They came with their children and stayed for several hours, talking, eating fruit, and drinking *sharbat*. It seemed they were consoled by listening endlessly to one another's complaints—about rising prices, the scarcity of jobs, the many young men who were killed in the war. Several of them had lost a relative or a friend. They hugged and kissed their children with an abundance of affection. They pampered Darius, who amused them with his broken Farsi and his American manner.

Sometimes men dropped in too. Hossein came once again, clearly, it seemed, to exchange glances with Zohreh. He told Jennifer that he had wanted to go to college but then he had had to serve in the army. Luckily he worked in a supply depot instead of actually fighting—having obtained that position through connections. After the war he had lost all motivation to go to school; now he owned a lamp shop.

Neither the men nor the women had gone beyond high school, and they all lived in this old-fashioned neighborhood, by and large untouched by the modernity the shah had introduced during his reign.

They reminded her somewhat of the people she had grown up with in Margaretville. Few of her high school classmates had gone on to college. They had stayed there, the girls getting jobs as waitresses, hairdressers, or secretaries until they got married, usually to local boys, and as soon as they had a child they quit their work. The boys became plumbers, electricians, mowed lawns, plowed the driveways of weekend houses, or they worked at the ski center or in lumberyards. Her own brother had gone into the lawn mowing business after high school and had built it up; now he was doing landscaping.

The visitors were cordial to her, but they did not understand, as Aziz and Monir did not, her need for work, for being alone sometimes.

If she withdrew into her room to try to do some work or just read, a novel she had brought with her or one that Zohreh had lent her, they seemed to feel hurt. Aziz would say to Monir, loud enough for Jennifer to hear, "What's she doing all alone in her room?" Monir would reply, "She must be sad." Then one of them would knock on the door. "Jennifer, Jennifer, is anything wrong, people want to see you, be with you." Once Jennifer had locked the door from the inside, an automatic, instinctive act, and Aziz had kept turning the knob, rattling it as if something were wrong. She had called, "Jennifer dear, are you there, are you all right?" as if she had been locked away for days, perhaps even dead. Another time she had heard Aziz say to Monir, "She comes from a different country. She has different ways of doing things. She can't help it any more than the cat can help having that color fur." Jennifer could see the merit of intense human interaction. Maybe it was better than the detached, cold attitude of the workaholics she knew in the United States, but still she yearned for periods of solitude.

Then there were *dowrehs* each woman in the family attended. Monir went to one with other women whose husbands had lost their jobs in the war. Zohreh had a book club, where they read mainly foreign novels in translation. Azar had joined a card-playing group. Aziz had a group of women friends who held prayer sessions monthly, each time in a different house.

Monir had told Jennifer that if she were there long enough she could go to a *dowreh* she knew of that consisted of foreign women married to Iranians.

"There are that many?" Jennifer had asked.

"Enough, I guess. Some of them must be Iranian by birth, but educated in Europe or America."

Then she had met one of those foreign women, an Austrian, married to an Iranian man. Britta had come over one afternoon with another woman who apparently was married to one of Aziz's second cousins. Britta stayed briefly and then invited Jennifer to visit her at her house. She said she had a little boy, only a year older than Darius; it would be good for them to meet.

Jennifer got out of the bed, thinking she would take Darius to visit Britta. She wanted to talk to her, and it would be good for Darius to meet another little boy.

Chapter 11

"How nice you came," Britta said, leading Jennifer and Darius inside. She introduced them to her other guests, two other women. Then she called to her son who was playing outside with other children.

Javad, dressed up in short pants and a starched, short-sleeved white shirt, looked prematurely grown-up for his age. He asked Darius to go out with him to play on the swing. Jennifer was happy to see that Darius's face brightened as he followed him.

The house, like the neighborhood, was relatively modern with an American-style kitchen and bathroom, but the furniture, except for a few pieces, was Iranian—Kashan rugs, brass-top tables. And Persian music was playing on a phonograph. "I'm swimming in the darkness of your eyes," a male voice sang. "I'm drowning in the memory of our love."

Other visitors were arriving by the minute, women with their children. The women took their chadors or scarves off, went into the bathroom, then came out with makeup on and their hair fluffed out. The children wandered into the courtyard while the women sat in the living room serving themselves tea, *sharbat*, fruit, and pistachios.

"You know, I'd never live in Austria again," Britta told her.

"Really, you like it here so much?"

"I was lonely there, people are so cold. It used to be great here with so many clubs—an American club, a French club, and an Austrian club. If I wanted to I could go visit people any time, play games—card games, tennis, Ping-Pong. Of course none of that exists now, so I try to provide a gathering place in my own house."

"How did you meet your husband?"

"I met him here. I was here with a group of other professionals from Europe to help set up a health clinic, one of the shah's projects then—by training I'm a social worker." She picked up a pomegranate from the platter of fruit on the table, cut it open with a knife, and began to eat the red seeds inside. She did it expertly, not allowing the juice to dribble down. "I quit working after I got married. Akbar wouldn't want me to work. It'd make him ashamed in front of his friends and family, it'd look like a commentary on his capacity to support his family. I used to think I had to have a career but to tell you the truth I feel good without it."

Jennifer noticed one of the guests looking at her. "Women are forced out of their jobs anyway," the woman said. "I used to teach computer science at a private school. Then there were complaints from the students' parents that a woman shouldn't be working side by side with men. Finally I was pushed out."

"The parents complained, even the mothers?" Jennifer asked.

"Many women here fully support what the new regime is imposing."

"I can see that," Jennifer said, thinking of Aziz, who unequivocally favored control by religious mullahs, and of Monir, who was not quite opposed to it.

"Of course there are some who're against it but they don't dare to express it."

Another young woman joined in. "It wasn't easy for women under the shah either. All the laws were still on the men's side. Boys inherited twice as much as girls from their parents, for instance. Men could divorce their wives with any excuse, but a woman had to prove a lot to get a divorce. Don't forget the shah himself divorced Soraya because she couldn't bear him a son."

They were interrupted by a shriek. A little boy had bumped into a chair and spilled a glass of *sharbat*. His mother jumped up and said, "Oh, no. Go on outside, will you." The boy dashed out. She went into the kitchen and came back with a sponge and tried to wipe off the sticky drink from the expensive-looking rug. After going back and forth a few times, she plopped into a chair, her eyes flaming, and said, "Where's their father? He doesn't even remember their ages. I've been pregnant as long as we've been married."

A young, teenage girl who had been sitting on the other side of the room came and sat next to Jennifer. She had very light coloring, fair skin, hazel-green eyes, and red hair. She would have been pretty if she had not been so thin and her face not so full of disturbance.

She asked Jennifer, "Are you American?"

"Yes."

"So is my mother." There was a sudden excitement in her voice.

"Really, does she live here now?"

"Oh, no, she lives in L.A. I've lived with my father most of my life, since I was ten years old. After my parents got divorced my mother went back home."

"Why didn't your mother take you?"

"She tried, I'm sure she did." Sadness spread over her thin, pale face. "In case of a divorce men get automatic custody of the children, that was true under the shah too."

Jennifer knew that but now here in Iran, the ominous implications hit her harder. "It's absurd, here women are the ones who sit home and take care of the children full-time," she said.

"But the men earn the living," Britta said mindlessly.

"They could give child support," Jennifer said.

"You just have to be careful not to get divorced in the first place," Britta said.

"Even if you're miserable?" Jennifer asked, with a flicker of annoyance at Britta's off-hand manner.

"You can always make a marriage work," Britta said.

Just then a man entered the room. "Oh, here's my father," the girl said, looking almost frightened.

"Please sit down for a while, if you don't mind an all-woman get-together," Britta said to him.

"I'll sit for a few moments." He stared at his daughter possessively. The girl introduced Jennifer to her father.

"Did Maryam tell you she was the first in her whole high school class last year?" he said to Jennifer. He had a nervous, overbearing manner, thinning dark hair, and a brush-shaped mustache. In contrast to his daughter, he was short and overweight. He went on, "I'm an artist . . . pottery . . . ceramics. My daughter is the brainy one."

Everyone was beginning to leave, whether because this man had descended on them or because they had to go, Jennifer could not decide. She got up too, in a dark mood, and went into the courtyard to get Darius. Darius was sitting by himself in a corner, not mingling with the other children.

Britta accompanied them to the outside door. "My husband and I are going away for a month to Europe for vacation but then I'll come over and see you."

"Yes," Jennifer said, more curtly than she intended.

Outside, she held Darius's hand, and they walked part of the way. The heat was not as oppressive as usual, with a breeze coming off the mountains and blowing away the stagnant air.

The day was long, endless. She asked Aziz if she could make an American meal for supper.

"You don't know how to use our unfamiliar kitchen," Aziz said.

"If you'd just show me how to use the stove."

Aziz did not resist this time. Jennifer thought she would make fried chicken, green peas and pearl onions, and mashed potatoes. She made a list of the ingredients and asked Aziz if they had any of them.

"I have everything," Aziz said.

The kitchen, a few steps down below the courtyard, was like a little cave, with jagged stone walls and low stone ceiling. Pots and pans were piled up on the floor. An old-fashioned, stumpy refrigerator and an old stove stood in one corner. Aziz showed her where everything was and how the stove worked.

Then Aziz actually seemed happy about Jennifer's offer and in fact she tried to make it into a real event. She took down the fancy china and silverware she kept on a top shelf in the kitchen and set them on the cloth.

The food tasted Iranian to Jennifer because of the spices she had to use in the breading, though to everyone else it was exotic.

Monir's attention was on her daughters as they ate. "Azar, you're getting a bit too thin," she said. "Zohreh, wipe that brooding look off your face," a remark that made Zohreh flinch.

After they finished eating, Aziz served fruit for dessert. Darius looked tired and cranky.

"My dear child, I promise to get you well," Aziz said to him in Farsi.

He was beginning to understand a lot already, with his grandmother tutoring him every day. At least that was something, Jennifer thought.

Zohreh and Azar went inside and in a moment the sound of American music was heard coming from their shortwave radio.

"What do they like about that music?" Aziz asked no one in particular. Then she got up and took Darius into her own room.

Jennifer told Monir about the young girl and her father she had met at Britta's house. Trying to see where Monir, who seemed to use her affability like a wall with her, really thought of such issues she said, "It's so hard here for women, particularly young girls."

"It's hard in some ways but easier in others. We're more protected than American women. We don't have to be out there making a living, dealing with job stress. I'm happy to raise my two daughters and, when we have a home again, to make it comfortable, beautiful," Monir said.

"Work can be exciting, fulfilling."

"My dear *khanoom*, we're from a different civilization, we go by different rules."

Jennifer wondered about Monir's relationship with Jamshid. She never stood up to him, though she was clearly intelligent and well-informed. She could talk about movies, plays, and novels, by both Iranian writers and foreign ones she had read in translation. Jennifer had a hard time believing that Monir was not oppressed by Jamshid, who was so demanding of her. His tea had to be just the right color or he would ask Monir to adjust it. He would not eat the stew if it was a touch overspiced. He liked his eggs, two of them, fried and turned over lightly so that the yolk was still runny but the white crisp at the edge—if they did not come out just right, he would ask Monir to make him new ones. He tended to be impatient, "What's taking her so long," he said, if Monir stayed a little longer than he expected in the kitchen before bringing out the food.

"How did you and Jamshid meet?" Jennifer asked.

"In Abadan. His mother is the one who spotted me on the riverbank, where my friends and I had gone after school, and her eyes kept following me. Finally she came up and asked for my address." A wistful expression came to her face.

"I guess you fell in love with each other afterward, once you got married."

"He's a good husband, a good provider," Monir said. "Love is an illness."

Jennifer was startled by that remark, then she thought, in a way it was accurate enough, it could take you over completely, blind you.

Monir got up and went inside. The alley cat wandered into the courtyard and sat by the pool. The fish began to dart around rapidly in the water. Jennifer thought of a vacation she and Karim had taken by a lake in Canada after they got married. They went fishing early in the afternoons and in the evenings Karim scaled the fish they had caught and broiled them on a charcoal grill. At night they slept in a tent they set up. One night as they lay there, kept awake by rain drumming against the tent, Karim said, "Nothing matters as long as we have each other."

They were so certain then that they could overcome any problems the future might bring. . . .

Chapter 12

"Aunt Jennifer," she heard Zohreh's voice from behind the door and asked her to come in.

"Do you want to take Darius to a playground?" Zohreh asked, coming in. "There's one in Shemiran, it's a long way to go, but it's a good one, it has all sorts of equipment."

She was not sure if it was a good idea for Darius to exert himself. He was getting worse. In fact he had a temperature of 100.5°F when she took it this morning. Nothing to be really alarmed about, it could be due to the heat, but still she could not stop worrying. She had asked Aziz and Monir if they knew a good pediatrician. "No," they both said. But then Monir had gotten a name for her from a friend. "Apparently he's American-educated and very popular," Monir said. Jennifer had gone out to the post office to call, since their phone was out of order, and the receptionist squeezed Darius in for the following day.

Getting Darius out would do him good, she decided. The three of them soon arrived at the playground, which was inside a small park and well-equipped, as Zohreh had said.

The park itself, carefully tended, was full of flowers. She encouraged Darius to join the other children in the playground. All the little girls were wearing *roopushes* and kerchiefs, giving them little more freedom of movement than if they were wearing chadors. The boys stood in clusters, separate from the girls, maybe instinctively or maybe because their mothers forced them. Darius, after standing alone for a while, joined the other boys in the sandbox.

Jennifer, curious about Hossein, the friendly young man who had come over to the house twice, asked Zohreh about him. "I guess you and Azar will both get married soon."

Zohreh did not answer immediately. Then she said, "There was someone Azar liked—he worked at the oil refinery in Abadan. But then we had to get out. Azar has no idea where he went, but I think he'll track her down."

"What about you? I liked that young man who came over."

"I don't want to be *forced* into marrying someone," Zohreh said.

Jennifer, fascinated by the idea of the arranged marriage, asked, "Aren't most marriages happy here, at least no less so than in the United States, where people choose their own partners?" In Iran parents not only selected someone for their children but supervised all the details to the end. The groom's mother would stand outside of the door of the room where the bride and groom withdrew after their wedding, and looked in to see if the bride behaved properly—she was not supposed to give in immediately to the groom's sexual demands, she should appear to be a virgin . . .

"Well, there's someone else I like," Zohreh said. She took out something from her pocketbook and held it in front of Jennifer. "The boy I like gave me this." It was a necklace, tiny hearts on a thin chain. "I can't wear it; I can't tell anyone about him and me. My father would kill me."

"Who's the boy, how did you meet?" Jennifer asked, surprised at Zohreh's secret life.

"I met him sitting on a park bench! He was with a group of other boys. He broke away from them and came and sat next to me. He studied in America, he's brilliant." She elaborated that he had a degree in communications and had been going to graduate school when he had a mental breakdown and was forced to come back home. The psychiatrist in Iran told him that his problem was due to his guilt that boys his age were fighting in the war and he wasn't. But ironically they didn't let him in the army because of his condition. "I like him because he understands my dreams of getting an education, being independent." Then all of a sudden she asked, "Are you a feminist?"

"I never did anything active, but I'd say so," Jennifer said. "Are you?"

"I believe in equality between men and women but we're so far from it here."

Darius came over and said, "Mommy, I'm hot."

They left the park and headed to the intersection to get a taxi. On the way they stopped at a stall and bought orange juice that the seller squeezed in front of them.

No taxis were stopping, so they went to the bus stop. Many people were waiting there already, some of them complaining about the heat. Jennifer was still thinking about the conversation she had had with Zohreh, when she became aware of a sudden hush. Then she saw what it was—a gray Paykan parked in front of them and three *pasdars*, all women, jumped out. They went directly toward a young girl, about Zohreh's age, standing in line with the others. Two of them held her arms and the other one pushed back her scarf and began to cut off patches of her hair with scissors.

"Oh, no, please stop," the girl began to scream. "Stop, stop."

All this happened so quickly that for a moment no one moved or said anything. Jennifer was frozen with shock. Both Zohreh and Darius were hanging on tight to her arms.

"Next time you'll be arrested," one of the *pasdars* said.

"What's the problem, she's wearing a scarf, isn't she?" one of the woman said to the *pasdars*.

"That's the way to wear it?" one of the *pasdars* said.

Then just as swiftly as they had come, without uttering another word of explanation, the *pasdars* got back into their car and drove away.

Darius was crying. "Look what happened," he said, pointing to the patches of dark hair on the ground.

Jennifer picked him up and held him in her arms, a difficult task with the chador.

The young girl whose hair was cut off was crying hysterically and the older woman who had spoken to the *pasdars*, was trying to comfort her. "The savages. Why did they do this to you? But don't worry, your hair will grow again."

The girl continued crying. "My hair, look what they did to it. I'm going to die, I want to die." She moved her body to and fro. She took a few steps as if about to run but then she stopped.

The older woman began to pick up the hair from the ground and put it in a handkerchief. "Here, keep this. Maybe you could make a wig out of it."

Several other women were looking sadly at the girl. "Just be careful next time," one of them said. "They're always looking for excuses to bother people."

"Mommy, why did they cut her hair?" Darius asked through sobs.

"They're poor, angry," Zohreh answered for her. She had gone dead white. "They're paid to do this."

The bus finally came and people rushed to get in. Darius leaned his head on Jennifer's arm, crying softly.

Chapter 13

At home, Monir, Azar, and Aziz were having their endless cups of tea, letting another day dwindle away.

"Well, well, back finally," Monir said.

"We were getting worried," Aziz said.

Darius went over to Aziz and sat on her lap, his face wet with tears. He clung to his grandmother and began to cry again. "What's wrong, my dear, what happened to you?" Aziz picked up some candies she had put in a bowl next to the bowl of rock sugar and gave them to him. "Here, this will make you feel better."

"Poor child was traumatized," Jennifer said. Now, at a distance, she could see the faces of the *pasdars* as if she were looking at a Polaroid photograph that was becoming clearer by the moment—they were full of humorless, cruel self-righteousness. "Some *pasdars* jumped out of a car and cut off a young girl's hair only because a bit of it was showing through her scarf."

"Like wild animals," Zohreh said, still looking distraught.

"No one bothers anyone if they're covered," Aziz said.

"In other countries people do as they please."

"Where did you get that idea?" Aziz said, indignantly.

Again Jennifer was aware of the weight of blame but to avoid an argument, she went inside. Zohreh followed her.

"We may go back home earlier than we'd planned," Jennifer said to her. "Depends on what the doctor says about Darius tomorrow."

"Oh, Aunt Jennifer, I wish you wouldn't. I like having you here so much. It isn't because of what happened today, is it?"

"I'm worried about Darius," Jennifer said, taking Zohreh's hand and squeezing it affectionately. Zohreh reminded her of herself as a teenager, full of rebellion and questions about the prescribed roles and attitudes she saw around her. "I should at least get our exit visas, so we can leave quickly if it comes to that."

"Sometimes they stamp 'No Exit Is Allowed' on your passport," Zohreh said. "Then you have no way of leaving, you'll get stuck in bureaucratic red tape for weeks and months."

"But on what grounds?"

"It's all arbitrary."

Zohreh was called by her mother and left but her words lingered in Jennifer's mind. "No Exit Is Allowed." It sounded like a nightmare.

At three o'clock, when the offices opened after a long midday siesta, Jennifer started to go to the passport office to at least find out what was involved. What she had told Zohreh about going back home earlier was growing more serious in her mind. Depending on what the doctor would say and on Darius's condition, she might really just leave. Karim, if he wished, could stay on until the time they had planned to leave. He had his own passport. Anyway, it was upsetting that he had left her and Darius here; he seemed to be taking his time with Jamshid. When things had been good between her and Karim, he had a hard time being apart from her even for a night; he liked to talk about everything with her daily. They called each other from work at least once a day and when working at home they took frequent breaks to compare notes, to discuss Darius. They usually reached an agreement on different issues, one of them giving in a little to the other, enough to satisfy both . . .

In the courtyard, Darius was sleeping on the rug with his grandmother's chador spread over him. Motionless, his hair matted down, he looked more like a bundle than a child sleeping.

"Going out again?" Aziz mumbled.

"I'm not a prisoner." Jennifer could not hold back her irritation.

"You do what you please and still . . ."

"You don't seem to mind your son always being out."

"He's a man."

"Just because he's a man he can do what he wants?" she said and rushed out.

The streets near the passport office were wide, tree-lined. She passed the mansion which had once belonged to the shah—it seemed to have been made into a religious school of some kind, there was a picture of a tulip on it, symbol of martyrdom. Slogans were painted on the walls: "Those who spread corruption on earth will be punished." "Think about God." "Iraq: puppet of the Great Satan, the Mercenary America." "Are we going to be trampled by boots of Americans because we have no dollars?" "America is run by mentally ill, perverted rulers, butchers, lechers."

She drew back in shock as she noticed an American flag painted in front of the entranceway for people to trample on.

The passport office was in a modern building. She rang the bell and she was buzzed in. Tables each with a sign above it were set in the lobby. She spotted the Exit Visa table and went over to it but no one was there to help her; the two chairs behind it were empty. She sat on the sofa along with other men and women waiting. Posters of mosques were hung on the walls. A potted rose tree stood in a corner. She could hear voices from inside of rooms.

"Excuse me, are you American?"

Jennifer turned to the woman sitting next to her, noticing that she looked American too. "Yes, from Ohio."

The woman's face brightened. "I'm from California. Are you having complications with your passport?"

"I need exit visas."

"Things can take months, if not years here."

"Years! Do you live here permanently?"

"Yes and no, not by choice."

Jennifer hoped for an explanation but the woman's expression was suddenly opaque. "I'd rather not go into it."

The door of one of the rooms opened, a man put his head out and called in English, "Pamela Adabi." The woman jumped up and started for the door. She paused half-way and said to Jennifer, "Good luck."

There was an impatient shuffle among the people waiting.

She herself could not sit still and kept shifting in her place. Maybe it was Darius's illness, or having spoken to the American woman, or the anxiety of complications in getting visas, but she suddenly was acutely homesick, missed her own family, even though she had never been all that close to them, except a little to her mother. Her brother had been the one who had stayed close to home. He had married a local girl, they had three children, and lived in a house in Margaretville. In other ways, too, Jim had duplicated their parents' lives—his wife was the one with the more formal education, she had a teaching certificate and taught in the high school, the same way their mother had been a nurse while their father had not gone beyond high school.

Jennifer could understand Karim's envy of her. In the United States she could just get on a plane and visit her family any time, while for many years it had been hard or impossible for him to do the same. Now the situation was reversed.

A young woman, wearing a kerchief and a long *roopush*, came out of a room and sat down behind the Exit Visa table and promptly started making a phone call. Jennifer went over to her.

"May I help you?" the woman asked when she finally got off the phone.

"I need exit visas for myself and my son."

"Can I see your passports."

Jennifer gave her the passports and the woman handed her a form to fill out.

The questions were routine: the length of the visit, the purpose of it. After finishing it she gave it back to the woman who looked at it perfunctorily, then turned to a calendar in front of her. Jennifer could see that the calendar was thoroughly marked with appointments.

"You can pick them up on August 28." She spoke in a laconic manner as if nothing of significance were going on.

"That's more than a month away! I may have to leave the country immediately, my child is sick."

"Madam, everyone who comes here thinks they have an urgent problem."

Then for no reason Jennifer could understand the woman's tone of voice changed. "If you get a doctor's permission that your son must see a specialist in America, then you can obtain exit visas much quicker."

"I'll see if I can do that, thank you," Jennifer said. The woman gave her a receipt for her passports.

When she got back Darius was in their room absorbed in looking at the pictures in a blue pamphlet.

"How do you feel?" She went over to him and put her hand on his forehead. He was still a little hot.

Instead of answering, Darius said, "Grandma said it's bad for you to go out alone." He spoke in that incongruously grown-up manner he had assumed at times lately. Just as disconcerting as when he regressed, clung to her, sucked his thumb.

"Did she? What are you looking at? Can I see it?"

He handed the booklet to her. "Path to God," was written on the jacket in Farsi. She turned to the first page. It showed a picture of a child looking at glowing sunrise. Underneath it said, "What is your goal? Are you looking for fleeting pleasures on this earth or are you looking toward the eternal life afterwards?" She closed the pamphlet and gave it back to him.

"Grandma says only praying will make me feel better." He went back to the pamphlet.

Chapter 14

"Damn it," Jamshid said, "Did you see how that car cut right in front of me? No one ever follows rules in this ruined, damned country."

Cars were coming at them from all directions at the intersection. It could take hours to go a few blocks, Karim thought. "Is there a way to avoid going through the town?" he asked.

"The back roads aren't in good condition. They're made for donkeys, not cars!"

There was a screeching sound, and then a strange, guttural moan from Jamshid as the car crashed into something, and came to a jerky stop. Karim gave a start as he saw blood trickling down the side of Jamshid's face. He was leaning on the wheel, breathing heavily, slowly.

"Jamshid, are you all right? Are you hurt?" Jamshid just moaned.

Some of the drivers had come out of their cars and were shouting and accusing each other. Several police cars and an ambulance appeared on the scene. Two men came out of the ambulance and went to the car next to theirs. They carried the injured driver, whose arm and face were bleeding, into the ambulance. Karim got out of the car. "Please help, my uncle has been injured too," he said to the ambulance men.

He helped them take Jamshid out of the car and put him in the ambulance with the other injured man.

"Where's the hospital?" he asked. "I'll follow you."

"On Martyred Hassan Avenue, that way, about fifteen blocks." The ambulance sped off.

One of the policemen who had been questioning someone in another car came over to Karim. "Is this your car?"

"No, it belongs to my uncle. He was taken away in the ambulance. I must get to the hospital."

"Can I see your license?"

"I have an international license. I'm visiting."

"Let me see it, and your passport."

Karim got his briefcase and took out his license and passport and handed them to the policeman who was now staring at him with a suspicious glint in his eyes. Then he walked around his uncle's car, inspecting it for serious damage, but there were only dents.

"What are you doing in Iran?" the policeman asked.

"Visiting my family."

The policeman wrote down some things and gave him back the passport and license. Then he asked more questions—how long did he intend to stay in Iran, how long had he lived in the United States.

Karim, more and more upset, got into the car and said, "I

must go." Other than for making a few odd sounds, the car seemed to be running normally.

Now looking at his own face in the mirror he saw a thin thread of dried-up blood on his temple. He tried to wipe it off with a tissue.

After an excruciatingly slow drive through the traffic he reached Martyred Hassan Avenue and turned into it. A small building with "Kholi Hospital" written on the canopy came into view. He brought the car to a stop close to the emergency entrance where several other cars and ambulances were parked.

In the lobby nurses were standing behind two counters. A sign on one said, "For Soldiers Only." Two soldiers were standing in front of that counter. One of them had his leg in a cast, the other had bandages on the side of his face and head.

Karim walked to the other counter and said to the nurse, "My uncle was just brought in here by an ambulance, he was in a car accident."

"His name?"

"Jamshid Soleimani."

The nurse checked a list. "He's in the intensive care unit."

"Can I see him or speak to his doctor?"

"I'll find out." The nurse walked down the corridor.

Karim went to the sofa and sat down. The afterimage of his uncle with blood trickling down his face wouldn't leave him. What will his family do if something happens to him? Of course I'll do my best for them. He remembered so vividly Aziz announcing Zohreh's and then Azar's births to him. "Your uncle had a baby, a girl." Each time she had hung lanterns on the tree branches and kept them burning for a few days in celebration.

Then he saw the nurse he had spoken to, accompanied by a doctor, approaching him and he got up.

"There was blood in his mouth that might be from an internal injury," the doctor said to him. "We'll have to keep him here under observation. He might have had a minor heart attack as well."

Karim thought about all the smoking, the stress his uncle had been under. "Can I go in and see him?"

"He shouldn't be disturbed right now. Come back tomorrow. It's lucky we have any space," the doctor said. "Every day they fly in soldiers still suffering from war injuries. Take care of yourself now." He walked away, then the nurse gave Karim some forms to fill out. It took Karim a long time—he had to think about certain facts, his uncle's exact age, for instance. He wrote fifty. He was not sure about his allergies, his history of illnesses. He left many of the questions blank. Then he went to the car and brought back his uncle's suitcase and gave it to the nurse with the forms.

He wondered what to do, where to go. He decided to go to his aunt's house anyway by himself.

"I haven't seen you for so long, I can't believe you're here," his aunt Khadijeh said as he stood with her and her son, Fereidoon, in the courtyard of their house. "We've all missed you so much."

"You know how impossible it was to get visas, but suddenly they made it easier, so we came."

"Did you come to Babolsar alone?"

"My wife and son are in Teheran, I came with Uncle. He had a job interview in Naushahr." He hesitated, then said, "Unfortunately we had a car accident. He's in the hospital right now."

"Oh, my God, what happened?"

"Don't worry, it isn't too serious . . ."

"Why is he in the hospital then?"

"Just to make sure he has no internal injuries."

"My poor brother, he's been through hell already."

Fereidoon said, "Why don't we go and see him?"

"Not today, they think he should be resting. But maybe tomorrow."

"Are you sure they won't let us see him?" his aunt asked.

"They want him to be quiet and rest."

His aunt sighed, a habit like his mother's. "I hope you'll stay a while with us."

"If I'm not imposing, coming here without notice."

"Of course not. You've become Americanized to ask such a question. Sit down, have some fruit."

Karim sat on the rug spread in the shade of a big fir tree.

Aunt Khadijeh took a pear from a platter heaped with fruit, peeled and sliced it, and put it on a plate for him. "The tea will be ready in a minute." She pointed to the samovar hissing, giving out sparks. Then she sank into silence, obviously upset about her brother.

Karim looked around. The house was as he recalled it—with the rooms on two floors, and there was an oval pool in the center of a brick-covered courtyard. The cobblestoned street had remained almost the same too—narrow, lined by houses with vines bearing gold or red grapes hanging over the courtyard walls.

"I'll go and buy chelo kebab for us," Fereidoon said.

"Please, I'm not hungry," Karim said. His stomach felt tight. "Do you by chance have a phone, or is there one nearby? I want to call Teheran."

"We don't have a phone, but the lines to Teheran are out again. At my shop we haven't been able to do any business for the last few days," Fereidoon said.

"It's the war. So many of our young men were dragged to the front and then killed. Practically every family in Babolsar has lost someone," Aunt Khadijeh said and sighed again.

"There are no winners in a war, both sides are losers," Fereidoon said. "They bribed families with promises of monthly payments and free education for their sons when they came home from the army. Some boys were simply taken away from their high schools and their families weren't told about it until much later. I was lucky, I managed to get out of the army because my mother is dependent on me—she has no husband and I'm her only child."

Somewhere in the distance beyond the house a radio went on, playing music. The water in the pool was perfectly smooth, reflecting the white, fluffy patches of clouds above.

"I guess it had some positive aspects for some of the young

men, the aimless ones. It gave them a sense of mission," Fereidoon went on. "But I have my work, and poetry."

"What kind of work do you do?" Karim asked.

"I transport fruit. I get up before dawn and go to the market to find the best fruit and then take it to different stores. My father did the same thing."

"I remember that," Karim said.

"One night a week I go to my poetry group—we recite poems by Khayyám, Hāfez, Saadi. Sometimes we play instruments—I play the lute."

Karim remembered writing poetry too when he was Fereidoon's age. One poem was about a boy standing at the bottom of a valley, surrounded by dark, tall mountains. "I am lost in the dark cloud of the unknown . . . ," or something like it.

"You look tired, do you want to lie down for a while and rest?" his aunt asked him.

"I'm sorry to be such poor company."

"We aren't strangers," his aunt said.

In a moment Fereidoon took him into a room. Together they spread a mattress on the floor and put sheets on it.

"Do you have a suitcase?" Fereidoon asked.

"Just a small bag, I'll get it later. I want to close my eyes for a few moments."

As soon as Fereidoon left the room, Karim fell asleep on the mattress with his clothes on.

Chapter 15

Dr. Bijan Daneshpoor's office was on the first floor of a small, two-story building on a busy street. On one side stood a tiny courtyard, filled with shrubbery and bushes, and on the other side, a bank.

As Jennifer entered the reception room, a nurse wearing a white uniform and a white kerchief that covered her hair completely approached her and asked, "May I help you?"

"I'm Jennifer Sahary, we spoke on the phone, this is my son, Darius . . ."

"Oh, yes, Sahary *khanoom*, please sit and wait, the doctor is with a patient, but he should be done shortly." The nurse's tone was very friendly. "You speak Farsi fluently."

Jennifer and Darius sat down and she filled out the form the nurse gave to her. There were many children in the room, some of them sitting close to their mothers, others standing around a fish tank in a corner. A sign on the wall advised, "Prevention Is The Best Weapon Against Illness." It was like any doctor's reception room in the United States.

In a few moments the doctor came out. His eyes focused on Jennifer. "Jennifer Sahary?"

"Yes, and this is my son Darius."

Darius leaned on her more closely.

"Let's go to my office."

A glass case in a corner of the office displayed old medical instruments, a hammer, a scale. A large print of Avicenna attending a patient hung on one wall and several diplomas on another.

"What's the matter with him exactly? Low fever, tiredness, anything else?"

"The fever comes and goes but in general he isn't himself, hasn't his usual energy."

"I'll give him some tests and see. By the way, your Farsi is excellent, I'm impressed." He had a boyish look, massive dark hair, lively eyes, and a casual, assured manner.

"My husband is Iranian."

"Still . . ."

Jennifer picked up the folded green robe from the table and helped Darius put it on. Then she stood there while the doctor examined him, looking into his eyes, ears, throat, taking his temperature, blood pressure, listening to his heartbeat. "His temperature is only slightly above normal right now," the doctor said. Then he took a throat culture. "Is he allergic to penicillin?"

"No," she said, helping Darius put his clothes back on.

"You're a nice, brave boy," the doctor said. He wrote a prescription and gave it to her. "Give him one of these four times a day until we know the test results, in two, three days."

She said to Darius, "Do you want to go out there and look at the fish?"

Darius left the office immediately and went over to the fish tank.

Jennifer turned to the doctor, "I have a favor to ask you, I may want to take him back home before we had planned, I need . . ."

"Why, you aren't happy here?" he said, touching her arm, his voice a bit flirtatious.

"It isn't that, I'm worried about my son. Anyway this isn't the best time for us to be here. I went to the passport office to get exit visas and they said it would take at least a month unless I had an urgent reason to leave. I told them my son was sick and they said if I could get a letter . . ."

"Wait here, I'll see what I can do."

He left the room and came back in a few moments with an envelope. "Here's the letter."

She was startled. "You already wrote it?" She took it out. On the top was the mandatory statement, "In the name of God, the Merciful, the Beneficent," and then,

> To whom it may concern,
> Darius Sahary has been my patient for the past three weeks. He has an obscure virus that most likely is caused by water, food, and air unfamiliar to the child. It is urgent for him to return to his native country, the United States, as soon as possible.
>
> Sincerely,
> Bijan Daneshpoor, M.D.

"I can't thank you enough," she said, putting the letter in her purse.

"I like to help when I can. Besides, I may need your help one day—a letter of invitation by an American is required for me to be able to obtain a visa to go to the United States," he said jokingly. "I'd like to go back and really live. All I did during the six years I was there was work."

The phone on the wall started to ring. He picked it up. "I'll be there as soon as possible." He put down the phone and turned to her, "An emergency. If you have any questions or need more help let me know." He walked with her to the door. As she was about to open it he leaned over and put his mouth to her ear and—it shook her—did he kiss it? "Come and visit me . . ." Did he really say that? She wasn't sure, she was feeling so nervous.

In the waiting room she said to the receptionist, "I can settle the bill now."

"The doctor gave me instructions not to accept any money."

On the way back she continued to wonder about the doctor, what kind of a person he was. He wasn't wearing a wedding band and there were no photographs of children, a wife, or anyone for that matter, in his office. But what difference does any of that make? Still, she could not suppress an attraction she felt, sparked by the kiss, or whatever it had been, in the middle of her turmoil. And his letter in her purse, an act of generosity no matter how she interpreted it, created a link, an intimacy.

On Jamali Avenue they went into the drugstore and filled the prescription, then they went to the toy store at the mouth of the alley, where she bought a yo-yo, crayons, a few coloring books, and a set of Chinese wooden eggs nested inside each other for Darius. In Athens, every Saturday, Karim used to take Darius to the hobby shop near the university and they picked out something. Then they'd come home and spend hours playing, putting together a train and its track, building a house with pieces that came in boxes. Karim also liked to measure Darius's growth every few months, making him stand against the wall, and then marking his height with a crayon. The marks were all there on the kitchen wall. They had made sure, when they painted the house, that they were left intact.

She felt a pressure in her chest. She had to suppress a desire to cry.

Chapter 16

While waiting for the passport office to open, Jennifer took Darius's and her own laundry into the courtyard to wash—the G.E. washing machine in the basement was broken, Aziz had told her, and parts were not available in Teheran. She put the clothes in a pan, added soap and water to it, and washed them by hand using a wash board. She hung them on a rope tied to two trees. She had found that she actually liked drying the clothes in the sun—they looked and smelled so good dried that way.

Darius was playing quietly in his grandmother's room, so she left without him. She found the same woman sitting at the Exit Visa desk and gave her the letter.

"Please wait," the woman said after reading it and wandered away to another room.

She came back and said, "Mr. Mobarek will see you now." She pointed the way.

Jennifer knocked at the door, and. after what seemed like a long time a man said, "Come in."

Inside she waited in the middle of the room, while the man behind the desk stared down at some papers. Finally he looked up and said, "Sit down." She sat across from him. His beady black eyes focused on her now, as he turned his diamond and sapphire rings around and around his fingers. The fragrance from the mint tea in a glass on his desk did not mask the cloying sweet smell of a cologne he was wearing. Two framed embroideries of the word "Allah" in large black letters on a green background hung on one wall. With the shutters pulled over the window and a lamp burning on the desk it looked like night in the room.

"What are you doing in Iran to begin with?" he asked.

"Visiting my husband's family."

"Do you have any documents with you to prove your marriage?"

From her purse she took out her marriage certificate, the one given to her by the Moslem priest, and handed it to him, thinking how lucky it was it had occurred to her to bring it to Iran.

The man looked at the document while he took sips of his tea. He left the room suddenly, and returned handing her the passports. "Are there exit visas on them?" she asked, confused.

He merely smiled at her in a strange, crooked way she could not understand the meaning of.

She opened the passports and looked. "No Exit Is Allowed," the phrase Zohreh had used, glared in her mind's eye nightmarishly before she actually saw that permission to leave had been stamped on both of them. Then she looked again to make sure.

When she got home Monir was sitting in the courtyard, ironing one of Jamshid's shirts on a flat board she had put on the rug in front of her. The electricity must have gone off because she was heating the iron on a coal stove. A spark came out of the stove and then faded. More clothes lay in a heap on the rug. For an instant Jennifer was hopeful that perhaps Karim and his uncle had returned. She asked, "Are the men back?"

Monir shook her head.

"What's taking them so long, I wonder."

Monir was her usual noncommittal self. She just asked, "Do you want me to iron some of your clothes hanging on the line, they should be dry by now."

"Thanks, you're very kind but I'll do them later myself. Is Darius still in his grandmother's room?"

"Aziz took him to Qom."

She stared at Monir. "Qom? That's two hours away."

"She wanted to take him to the shrine and pray for his recovery."

"She took my sick child away without my permission. When did she say they'll be back?"

"Qom has a very special religious school for children. She thought it would be good for him to attend it for a couple of weeks."

"A couple of weeks! I can't believe it. He's sick. Why didn't she ask me?" For an instant it was as if the whole world had faded away, its edges dissolving, she felt so unsteady and lost.

"Don't worry about it, Darius was happy to go."

"How can you say that? But you'd take her part, you and Aziz are such good friends. I'm just an outsider."

"She's being kind to us, putting us up all these months and she's the oldest member of the family. In Iran we respect old people."

"Yes, of course, but that doesn't give her the right to take my child away. I have to go there at once and get him. Where are they staying?" She was breathing with difficulty.

"With her cousin, Batul *khanoom*."

"I'll take the bus there right now."

"No buses at this hour. There are a few early in the morning, then one at noon, and one at three thirty."

"Are you sure there isn't one later than that?"

"I'm sure."

"Do you know anyone who'd drive me there? Of course I'll pay him."

For the first time Monir looked impatient. "How am I going to find someone?"

"I could take a taxi . . ."

"Taxis won't go that far unless you've arranged it in advance. Anyway it wouldn't be safe for you to be alone in a taxi for such a long distance, particularly with your blue eyes. You don't need to go there today!"

Jennifer could not stop a sick, sinking feeling. Everything was sliding out of her control. Now Aziz's behavior yesterday took on a new meaning: The resolute way she went about her tasks, avoiding conversation or eye contact with anyone, the way she was mumbling about the medical profession being backward. In her outrage Jennifer could not summon up tolerance for Aziz—she was a self-absorbed, selfish woman. What she had done amounted to kidnapping. "I can't take this, nothing makes sense," she said. "I've really had it. First Karim goes away and stays away as long as he likes, and now Aziz has taken Darius to another town without saying a word to me about it."

"Please don't worry," Monir said. "Come and sit down here, I'll get you something to drink."

Jennifer ignored that. Entering her empty room, she was hit by a great loneliness. Darius's grown-up-looking imitation leather slippers that Aziz had bought for him were flung on the floor, one by the bathroom door and one upside down by the bed, his toys were strewn on the floor and his bed was unmade. She could no longer stop herself, she began to sob. She went into the bathroom, shut the door, and kept crying. She said to herself inwardly, stop being frantic, he can't be that sick or else he would have a higher temperature, wouldn't be able to get out of bed at all, it's bound to pass, but she couldn't push away the weight pressing on her chest.

After she calmed down a little she looked in the medicine cabinet to make sure Aziz had taken the penicillin with her. She didn't find the jar there, so she went to Aziz's room to check there. The air had a lingering scent of the rose water Aziz spread on her chadors and dresses before she went out. She looked on the shelves and then the mantle but she could not find the medication. She noticed that Aziz, as if propelled by a new energy, had put on the mantle the framed portrait of the prophet Mohammed as a young man with a halo around his head that she had seen before in the basement and next to it a photograph of Darius as a toddler they had once sent to her.

At least Aziz seemed to have taken the penicillin. She kept trying to think of a way to get to Qom that day but then she realized Monir was right, she had no choice but to wait until morning.

Chapter 17

I have nothing against medication and doctors, they are created for humans by God, but these penicillin pills are making him worse, Aziz thought, throwing the jar into the river. The river was almost down to a trickle. Some women were washing clothes and rugs in it and then spreading them out on the rocks. Aziz loved the river, the hills around Qom, the startling greenness of the orchards against all the aridness.

Then, holding Darius's hand, she went toward the shrine. Nothing helps as much as prayer, she thought. It was prayer that saved Karim when he was a child from dying in a typhoid epidemic that killed hundreds of children. She could almost see herself as a young woman, holding Karim by the hand just as she did Darius now, coming to Qom to pray for his recovery. Under the chador, she remembered clearly as if it were yesterday, she was wearing her blue satin dress and a blue ribbon on her hair. She was pretty, she knew, everyone said so. They said she was the pretty sister, Khadijeh was the vivacious one. Youth passes so quickly. She could never forget the closeness, all the sharing and confiding she had done with her sister and brother when they were children. Not that they were not close now, but being older, having lived through so many different concerns and experiences, made the closeness bittersweet. They had been lucky in many ways, though. They all married well and had wonderful children, though she had wished for more. Karim seemed to have the same fate now, for he and Jennifer appeared to be unable to have more children.

What does Jennifer know about the healing power of prayer? She isn't a bad person and she is so pretty, like a china doll, but she's inscrutable in some ways. She will never blend in with us, she *keeps* herself separate, independent, from us. How do she and Karim fit together, two such different people, or has Karim become like her in ways I cannot see? If only she would live on in Iran instead of taking my son and grandson away from me again, I would lavish her with so much love that she would change to our ways. She is more simple and naive in certain ways than many Iranian wives can be.

The shrine stood among several religious colleges and institutes. They entered its building through the gateway and then went into the huge first courtyard, facing the enormous gold dome and minarets and arches above the shrine. The intricate patterns made by pieces of mirrors cut to fit the honeycomb surface inside the three arches was such an amazing sight. Its splendor never diminished in her eyes, no matter how many times she came there.

Families with children were sitting in the courtyard, picnicking, finches hopping around tree branches above them.

She and Jamshid and Khadijeh were taken to this shrine frequently by their mother. Their mother and father were buried in Qom in a graveyard not far from here. She would go and pay a visit in a day or two after Darius was well, show him the graves of his great-grandparents. He was so curious about everything, and so smart. He was already learning Farsi and prayers so quickly.

They went up onto the porch and she bought candles from an old man with a full white beard. Then she checked Darius's and her own shoes with another man who stood inside a cubicle. She paused to kiss the door of the shrine and asked Darius to do the same. Darius said, "I don't want to." They went through the anteroom, then to the main room where the tomb stood. She lit candles among the others already burning in the small chamber on the side of the sarcophagus. Many pilgrims were standing around the tomb, pleading, praying. Some of them threw coins on the tomb through the silver grating surrounding it. Scents of sandalwood rose from the coffin inside. The words of prayers and of Koran *surehs* echoed all around, penetrating her so deeply that soon it was as if they were coming from inside her. Bowing toward the sarcophagus she whispered, "I have tried to be good, I have prayed every day, given alms to the poor. I beg you, the Merciful, to make my only grandson healthy, immune to diseases. I have been teaching him to pray, please guide my only grandson to the right path, and to health." As she stood there with Darius, her arms around him, praying with her eyes closed, everything began to glow brightly, penetrating her shut eyelids. Then she thought she heard a voice, serene and holy, coming from the sarcophagus and spreading through her, "Your wish has been answered." For an instant she felt such a unity with the saint that she would not mind her life ending at that moment, then she came to herself and she thought of Darius and her responsibility toward him.

She was filled with happiness, hope, as she walked back with Darius, into the anteroom, and then went into a smaller room that was for women only. Darius was just young enough to be allowed in the all-woman room. She sat down on the rug to rest her aching knees and let Darius stretch out beside her. She covered him except for his face with a part of her *chador*.

Other women were sitting there also, alone or together, talking. A woman came in and began to pass around food—dolmas, dried fruit. "I'm here to beg Saint Fatemeh to give my daughter a baby. She's been trying for years, with no success."

I should bring food here too, Aziz thought. I'll come back for that on another day. Conversation buzzed around her. "I think my husband has another wife," one young woman was saying. Another one said, "Let him, he'll bother you less." Two other women were talking about a relative who had cancer.

Another woman came by passing glasses of tea and rock sugar around. Aziz took a glass for herself and one for Darius, who was waking up, and rock sugars, too, for both. She put the hard pieces of sugar in the glasses and stirred them until they dissolved. She urged Darius to drink some. "It's good for you." Darius took a few sips and then pushed away the glass.

She drank her own tea quickly, thinking they should get going. This was a good time to find Batul *khanoom* home.

Outside she said to Darius, "I want you to start the *maktab* tomorrow. You'll learn a lot that's good for you, my dear child, that will lead you to heaven."

"Can I swim in heaven? And eat ice cream all I want?"

"Of course. Anything you ask for, and in the most beautiful of places." She marveled once again at how well Darius had understood her and how well he had answered.

She stopped at the grocery store and bought quince jam, yogurt, and bread for Batul *khanoom* and dried apricots, peaches, and cherries for Darius. "Already you're feeling better, aren't you?" she said to him.

He just pouted his lips.

Chapter 18

Jennifer had a hard time sleeping when she went to bed. She stared at the faint patterns of light from the lanterns in the courtyard skipping around in the room. When she finally fell asleep she kept waking up from disturbing dreams. In one, she and Darius were standing by a pool in their bathing suits. Darius jumped in first, then he called in a high, tinny voice, "Mommy, Mommy, come in." As Jennifer was about to go in, the air became hazy and then pitch-dark. The pool receded into darkness.

In another one, she was in a dark alley and she could hear Darius calling in a clear, glass-sharp voice. "Take me with you."

"Where are you?" she asked, starting to run.

"Mommy."

Then she saw Darius standing in a doorway, naked, his stomach bloated, his eyes bright and blinking like a kewpie doll. She got out of bed at dawn and quickly packed an overnight bag for Qom, in case she couldn't return that day.

She could hear footsteps in the courtyard, the clatter of dishes. No matter how early she woke others were already up before her, to do their prayers or set up the samovar.

"Don't you want any breakfast?" Monir asked her as she entered the courtyard.

"I'll get something at the station. Aziz's cousin's address is twenty-two Dadghar Street?" she asked to make sure she recalled correctly the address Monir had given her last night.

Monir nodded. "Easy to remember, just ask anyone, they'll tell you where the street is. But be careful, Qom is a very conservative town. Do you know what the saying is about it, they export religion and import the dead."

Jennifer tried to smile.

Monir elaborated, "Almost all mullahs are graduates of Qom's theological schools. And people like to bury their dead there, so that their graves are near the shrine of Fatemeh."

Before going to the bus station Jennifer stopped on Yusef Abad Avenue and went into the foreign currency exchange shop. She was running out of *toomans*. Luckily it was already open at that early hour. She gave the man in charge two one-hundred-dollar bills and received a huge stack of *toomans* in exchange.

The station was very crowded but several buses were going to Qom and she had no trouble buying a ticket. Then she bought tea, cheese, and bread at a stall and ate them quickly. Her bus started boarding. As she was getting on she saw "Death to America" written in large black letters on the side of the bus. The slogan, though pervasive, always made her uneasy. And now she was feeling more vulnerable than usual, maybe because of Monir's warning.

The bus was filled to capacity. Some of the passengers were forced to put their luggage next to them on the floor. Children sat on their mothers' laps. The driver took his seat and said, "In the name of God." Several passengers repeated, "In the name of God." The woman sitting next to her was reading a newspaper. Jennifer glanced at the headlines and main stories, "*Ayatollah* Bagi's message: Once again I remind everyone of the festering, cancerous American tumor growing in Islamic countries. It is our duty as Moslems to eradicate the tumor by spreading the revolution. . . ." "Yesterday tens of thousands of people demonstrated in front of the former Nest of Spies, the American Embassy . . ." She turned to the window.

Except for patches of wild flowers in bright red, purple, and yellow appearing now and then, the landscape was arid along the roads they traveled. The shadows on the ground were dark and wide. They passed a lake. The driver said, "That's the salt lake the shah's secret police threw people into. They were thrown in alive with their hands tied up." A hum of horror rose from the passengers.

As they approached Qom a glittering golden dome became visible between two minarets.

The driver brought the bus to a halt on a narrow dirt road next to a food stall and a gas station. "Last stop," he said, "We're in the holy city of Qom."

There was a wild rush among the passengers to get off.

Some of them went to the stall to buy food, others took their children to the public bathroom behind the station.

As Jennifer picked up the bus schedule for her return trip to Teheran, she asked a woman who was standing by the stall eating a large slice of watermelon, "Do you know where Dadghar Street is?"

"Walk straight ahead. See that blue dome? When you reach it, look for Dadghar Street. It's about twenty or thirty blocks from here."

Jennifer began to walk straight ahead. The streets were as noisy and crowded as in Teheran and dustier, the houses older, more squalid, but then on almost every block there were beautiful mosaic-covered buildings and mosques.

Her way was obstructed for a moment by a crowd that had gathered around a man playing the flute and a large cobra twisting its long body rhythmically to the music and waving its tongue in the air. Children jumped up and down and gasped in excitement as the snake raised its head very high and then lowered it again. The snake's yellow brown skin gleamed in the sunlight, its movements hypnotizing.

Along the way a group of young men and women rushed out of an alley, some of them holding a banner in front of them, "Death to the Satanic West."

Two men walking ahead of her were talking about chemical bombs. "They get blisters all over them and then cough, they cough blood. Blood seeps out of their skin."

"Stop *khanoom*, stop," Jennifer heard an unfamiliar male voice from behind her, then a man came forward and stood in front of her, blocking her way. Another man and two women joined him. *Pasdars*. Her heart sank.

"You're flaunting your hair," one of the men said, staring at her.

The horror of the scene she had witnessed by the bus stop in Teheran rushed back to her. Nervously she put her hand on her forehead and then pulled her chador over a patch of her exposed hair.

"Your name?"

She felt faint. Should I make up a name, should I let them know I'm an American?

"Your name?" he asked again.

"Jennifer Sahary," she said finally.

"American?"

Again she hesitated.

"American," he concluded. "What's your purpose in Iran? You know the language."

"I came to Iran with my husband and son to visit his family."

"You have to come with us for further questioning." He pointed to a gray Paykan.

"I don't understand, for what?" She was becoming more faint. She had an urge to shout for help.

"Get in or else we'll have to force you."

Passersby stared at them furtively but no one paused.

"Go on," the *pasdar* said.

She walked toward the Paykan. "I'm in Qom to pick up my son, he's here with his grandmother, he's sick . . ."

But the man opened the back door, pushed her inside, and got in next to her. One of the women squeezed in with them. The other *pasdars* sat in front.

"Where are you taking me? I haven't done anything," Jennifer protested. No one bothered explaining. "Please take me to where my son is with his grandmother."

The driver parked the car, not by a police station but, to Jennifer's amazement, by a mosque. She followed them out of the car and into a courtyard faced by a row of rooms on each side. Prayers were going on in one of the rooms, shoes piled up in front of it. A large group of women was sitting in a circle around a mullah who was giving a sermon.

The *pasdars* led her into another room. "Sit down," one of the men said to her.

She sat on the rug on the floor and then, one by one, the others did too.

"You have to explain to Ayatollah Negari what you're doing here in Qom."

"Why are you really in Iran?" one of the women asked. "Are you collecting information?"

Four pairs of eyes were fixed on her.

"I told you, I came with my husband and son to visit, it's as simple as that."

They looked at her skeptically.

"I spent a year in Rolla, Missouri, at the School of Mines. I wanted to become an engineer but I gave up the idea. Your people persecuted me because of my skin color," the man who had questioned her said grimly, though his skin was not much darker than hers. He was very tall, broad-shouldered, and had piercing dark eyes. His sheer size made him menacing.

Jennifer was silent. She had a helpless feeling that ordinary words would not reach these people. Would they take a bribe, she wondered. She had some jewelry and cash on her. "Can I give you a . . ." She was not sure how to word it. "A present?"

One of the women said stiffly, "We don't take bribes."

They all gave her contemptuous glances. The tall *pasdar* got up restlessly and went to the doorway. He stood there for a moment and then came back. Addressing the other male *pasdar,* he said, "The ayatollah must have been called away somewhere. Shall we take her?"

"Where?" Jennifer asked.

"Jail. You'll be held there until tomorrow, the ayatollah should be able to see you then."

"This is absurd." Her voice was barely audible to herself. This can't be really happening.

"Let's wait another hour," one of the women said.

"Can't you let me go?" Jennifer said, and again, "You must take me to where my son is staying . . . please . . ."

No answer. Jennifer remembered the advice the school counselor had given her when she was going through a bad period in college: "As soon as a disturbing thought comes into your mind, try to replace it with a positive one." Now, as if she were a young girl again, she tried to do that. But it was hard to conjure up anything positive. All she felt was a knot of anger and fear.

Chapter 19

Jennifer fidgeted anxiously as she sat trying to anticipate the ayatollah's questions. Why are you in Iran? For how long? Do you have a mission? Answer him minimally, let him do most of the talking, she decided.

One of the women got up and left the room. In a moment the two men left also, without explaining where they were going. The only *pasdar* remaining with her went to the mantle and came back with a wicker fan. She began fanning her face. "I can't bear this heat," she said. After a pause she added, "The ayatollah will want to know if you accept Islam."

"I'm a Moslem, through my husband," she said, to appeal to the woman's sympathy. But the Moslem wedding ceremony, now that she thought back on it in this atmosphere, weighed heavily on her, as if she had accepted a dogma, a force, designed to oppress women.

The *pasdar* was staring at her. "Why do you, in America, need so much?" she asked. "So many things, so many useless luxuries; they snuff out a person's soul."

"I could live without most of them myself," Jennifer said, thinking how much she liked the sparseness of furnishing in Aziz's house and in this very room, with only a single intricately designed rug on the floor and two large potted plants set near the doorway.

A faint smile appeared on the woman's face but she did not say anything.

Jennifer was quiet too, staring at the rug. The mineral and vegetable coloring used in it had softened by age to sea green and pale blue. The lotus-shape medallion at the center was filled with roses and lilies, matching the floral designs at the edges of the rug. The flowers, stylized and delicate, were surrounded by abstract forms that could be foliage or mist or fire.

The other woman came back in. She was carrying bottles of *doogh* and glasses. With a self-righteous look, she gave each of them a bottle and a glass. Jennifer drank hers quickly, she was feeling dehydrated. "What happened to the ayatollah?" Her voice was drowned out by a hum of voices flowing in from the room where the sermon was taking place. It seemed the sermon was over and the women attending it were talking among themselves. An airplane roared in the sky. When she was younger, Jennifer remembered, that sound made her yearn to travel, go to faraway places, experience new things. Now she was overwhelmed by a desire to be back home, in her own house with its green surroundings.

An idea was hazily forming in her mind and then it became more clear. If I could find some excuse to go to the courtyard I could hide among the women as soon as they come out of that room and leave the mosque with them. She surveyed the courtyard, then turned to the *pasdar* she had been talking to. "I have to use the toilet, could you tell me where it is?"

The *pasdar* looked perplexed as if confronted by a huge problem she hadn't anticipated. Then she said, "I'll take you there."

"You don't have to come." She tried to sound mild, offhand.

"But I must." The *pasdar* started to go outside in a choppy, graceless way and Jennifer followed.

Jennifer looked toward the room full of women and an *aghound*. He was holding a glass of tea, drinking it. The timing is wrong, she thought, despair washing over her. She asked the *pasdar* faintly, "Won't you let me go, please?"

The *pasdar* raised her eyebrow dramatically and then gave a shrill little laugh. "You really think I can just let you go?"

When they reached the bathroom door the *pasdar* said, "I'll wait for you here. I want to smoke a cigarette in the fresh air." She began to rummage through the large pocket on the side of her uniform.

Jennifer was astounded that this stern woman would indulge in a frivolous pleasure. Anyway she hoped she had caught her doing something wrong. "Is a woman allowed to smoke?" she asked.

"Why not? It isn't against Islam," the *pasdar* said with annoyance as if Jennifer had displayed terrible ignorance.

Inside the bathroom Jennifer immediately noticed an open window with a thin curtain covering it. She pulled the cloth aside and looked out. The window was not more than a few feet above the ground. Except for a beggar sitting against a wall, the alley was empty. Without hesitation, she climbed up to the ledge of the window but it was difficult to jump out with the chador on. She took it off, folded it around her overnight bag and purse, and threw the bundle down into the street. Then she jumped, feet first.

A sharp pain shot up her legs and hips as she landed, but ignoring that, she quickly picked up the bundle, unwrapped the chador, and put it on. The beggar looked at her in a detached way, without saying anything.

Jennifer glanced in both directions, wondering which way to turn. Just then the women who had been in the room inside, at least fifty of them, all in black chadors, rushed into the alley from the back door of the mosque. Reflexively, Jennifer joined them. For a brief moment she felt lightheaded, daring, before the fear of being caught began to take over. She glanced nervously toward the window through which she had escaped. No one was looking out of it. The *pasdar* must be still smoking her cigarette. Jennifer held the chador tightly around her face and kept her eyes downward as she walked with the women.

When they reached the wide avenue running perpendicular to the alley, the women began to disperse, in different directions. Jennifer walked rapidly as she kept looking for a taxi but the few she saw zoomed by without stopping. The avenue was congested with heavy traffic, zigzagging, honking. She was almost choking from the cars' exhaust fumes. An old bus rumbled down the street and stopped near her. She climbed in, paid the fare, and went all the way to the back.

In about twenty blocks she got off the bus and looked around fearfully, wondering which way to go to avoid being caught by the *pasdars* who might be looking for her by now. She started walking on the main street, thinking she would be able to hide there among the large number of pedestrians passing by. After a few blocks she spotted the blue dome and went in its direction, checking the names of the side streets. She was full of longing for Darius, as if she had been apart from him for weeks. She yearned to be in a cool and comfortable place to rest a while, take a shower to clean off the dust and sweat. "Dadghar," was written on a blue tile on the top of the wall at the beginning of a cobblestoned street. She turned into the street and looked for number twenty-two, but most of the houses had no numbers on them. A man was squatting by the *joob*, washing his face. She asked, "Do you know the house belonging to Batul *khanoom* on this street?"

"Batul *khanoom?* Over there." He pointed to a house, a few feet away, with a crude brick and straw wall around it.

"Thank you," she said.

She went to the house and knocked. She realized she was trembling, feeling the delayed impact of having been arrested. I could have been locked up in jail with no one knowing my whereabouts, she thought, for days, months. It's incredible I actually escaped.

An old, stooping man opened the door. "Yes?"

"Is Batul *khanoom* in?"

"No one is home. They all went out."

"Darius too?"

"He's at the *maktab*."

"I'm Darius' mother . . ."

"Oh, his mother, come in, come in and have some tea," the old man said, his face brightening. "He's going to be happy to see you. He was crying this morning, asking for you."

"He was crying for me? Where's the *maktab?*"

"See that mosque, the *maktab* is inside of it." He was pointing to the blue dome, visible above the walls of the neighboring houses.

She took out fifty *toomans* and gave them to him. Behind him she could see a garden with several flower beds filled with rosebushes, snapdragons, asters. How ordinary and beautiful the sight was and how pleasant this simple old man, she thought, and I am out of the grip of those *pasdars*, very close to my son. But still she could not relax, be free of her anxiety. She started going toward the *maktab*, crossing from one side of the street to the other to be in whatever shady spots she could find.

Chapter 20

"Jennifer," Karim called. "Jennifer." He moved his hand gently on her breasts, stomach. "Jennifer, don't you hear me, Jennifer, Jennifer?" Why was she so silent? He leaned over and kissed her lips. He bit them, hoping for a response, but her lips were cold and still. He stared at her face and waited for her to smile, to say that it was all a joke. My God, this isn't Jennifer, it's an imitation, oh, God, what happened to her? His heart was pounding when he woke. It took him a moment to realize he was in his aunt's house and then he recalled his uncle's accident.

He lay there, unable to shake himself from the mood of the dream. What was this abyss now between him and Jennifer? They had been so much in love. Meeting her had transformed him, uplifted his whole life, it had seemed at the time.

Finally he got out of bed and began to dress. The oval window cast a rose-purple-amber rainbow on the rug. The antique clock chimed the hour. Through the lacy curtains he could see the garden—the yellow grapes on the arbor, the pomegranates bright in the sun, and Fereidoon throwing seeds on the ground and hens and roosters pecking at them. It was under the grape arbor, Karim remembered, that he had sat as an adolescent and written a poem.

He had taken little Fereidoon on walks, played ball with him, helped him fly a kite in the fields. In early mornings he would watch his aunt make yogurt and cheese.

He left the room and went into the courtyard.

"Do you feel better?" Fereidoon asked him.

"Yes, thanks, it was good to get some rest." He went outside to get his stuff from the car. He took his overnight bag out of the trunk, then he looked in front for his briefcase. It wasn't there. He looked under the seats. Nothing. What could have happened? Could someone have stolen it? Perhaps he hadn't put it back in the car after he showed his passport and license to the police. He'd been so distracted that he might have just left it on the ground. It had all his important documents in it. To obtain a new Iranian passport would take months.

Back at the house he said to Fereidoon, "I can't find my briefcase. Either someone stole it from the car or I left it at the side of the road."

"No one ever steals around here. Why don't we go back to look for it? We can take my truck."

Karim could almost see his briefcase lying on the ground with cars passing it by, but when they got to the scene of the accident, there was no sign of it. They decided to check at the shops lining the sidewalk to see if anyone there had spotted it and brought it in.

"Did you by chance see a briefcase lying on the street over there?" Fereidoon asked as they went from one shop to another.

"You could call the police station," the owner of a kilim shop, a short, fat man, said. "Use my phone. It's working."

Fereidoon got the police precinct's number from information and dialed. "It's busy." He waited and tried again until he finally got through. "Did anyone turn over a briefcase to you? It was left on the ground in the main intersection, yes, there was an accident. . . . I'll check with you again later . . ."

Karim thought he would try calling Teheran and he was surprised that someone picked up. "Hello, this is Karim," but only a blast of static reached him, drowning out the voice on the other end.

He hung up and tried again, "This is Karim, do you hear me? Do you hear me, Karim . . ." This time unfamiliar voices came onto the line, two women were talking about a wedding.

He gave up. He put down a few *toomans* on the desk for the owner.

"Have you just returned home from abroad? You have a different way of speaking," the man said.

"Yes, I live in America."

"I've never left Babolsar. It has all I want."

"You're lucky to be where you want to be." The man invited them to have tea. He went to a cubicle and came back with a tray holding tea glasses and sugar. Then while Karim and Fereidoon drank their tea, he unfolded some of the kilims on the floor for them to see.

"They're very nice. Maybe we'll come back and I'll pick one," Karim said.

In a moment he and Fereidoon thanked the man and left, Karim was anxious to get to the post office and send a telegram to Jennifer. He thought about wording the letter so that it would explain the delay without throwing everyone into a panic. ". . . We had an accident, are staying at my Aunt Khadijeh's house until we get the car fixed. I hope Darius is all better by now. Send a telegram to Khadijeh's address if you want to reach me." He added the address.

After the post office they went to the hospital to check on Jamshid. The nurse told them he was making remarkable progress but the doctor thought it was too soon for him to have visitors or go home. They could return tomorrow.

They strolled the streets for a while and then went to a bazaar, a huge labyrinthine place with myriad shops displaying gold, clothing, leather goods, carpets, fabrics, copper and silver, and many other types of merchandise. War had damaged sections of it but it still was functioning. As dusk approached Karim bought dinner from a chelo kebab restaurant to take home to his aunt. They ate in the courtyard, lit by a lamp and a full moon dangling close to the fruit trees.

Later as Karim took a shower in the tiled covered bathroom in the courtyard, with the moon and the stars winking at him, he felt an intense happiness—as if nothing mattered other than the beauty of this moment.

Chapter 21

Jennifer opened the intricately latticed metal gate of the mosque and went inside. For an instant she was distracted by the beauty of a wall at one side of the courtyard, covered with tiles, each with a peacock design on it. On the other side stood a row of rooms, but only one of them showed signs of life, with voices coming from it. As she went closer she could see, through its half-open door, a group of children sitting cross-legged on a rug and a woman in the middle of the room facing them, a large Koran on a wooden lectern open before her. She was reading lines from the Koran and the children were repeating them after her. Jennifer felt a pang in her heart as she spotted Darius, who looked lost and confused. She knocked on the door and the teacher motioned to her to wait. She stood there, trying to control her impulse to walk in and snatch Darius away. She waved at him, but he didn't see her.

She couldn't bear waiting. She knocked again. The teacher came to the door. "Yes?" She wore a gloomy expression, accentuated by her all-black clothes.

"I'm Darius's mother."

"His mother?"

Jennifer was aware of being scrutinized by the woman.

"Mommy, Mommy." Darius had gotten up and was coming toward her. Jennifer picked him up in her arms and kissed him. His skin felt hot. He clearly had fever. Fear shook her.

"I'm going home with my mommy," Darius told the teacher.

"Do your prayers at home properly," the teacher said to him, and then to Jennifer, "Will you make sure he does?"

Jennifer ignored that and walked with Darius to the gate. Her throat was constricted, her knees weak. As she reached the gate she glanced back at the teacher hovering in the doorway, watching them.

She paused at the busy main street and looked at the bus schedule back to Teheran. Shoot, she had just missed the 4:30 bus, the last one today. She decided to check into a hotel for the night. If she went back to Batul *khanoom*'s house some argument or resistance on Darius's or Aziz's part could create obstacles. Meanwhile she had to get something to bring down his fever. "Did your grandma give you the pills I got for you?" she asked him.

"No."

Maybe he didn't remember or the pills weren't working or Aziz had not given them to him. Could she possibly get some without a prescription if she convinced a pharmacist that Darius had fever? She noticed a drugstore nearby and went in.

A middle-aged, stern-looking man was standing in the back. She said to him urgently, "My son has fever and I don't have the penicillin his doctor prescribed for him with me. Is it possible for you to give me some without a prescription until I see his doctor again tomorrow?"

"'How could you forget his medication?" the man accused her.

"I didn't forget, please can we have . . ."

"Let me see." He got a thermometer and took Darius's temperature. "He has fever all right." He disappeared for a moment and returned with a jar. "Here are a few pills. Take the thermometer too." He was staring at her. "Are you Russian?"

She hesitated. "Yes, thank you so much for your help." As they waited by the curb for a taxi or a bus to come by, the nightmare of the *pasdars* swept over her again. She pulled the chador over her face so tightly that even her eyes were almost covered. Behind them stood a public bath with a loincloth hanging on the door, where men with wet hair and flushed cheeks were going in and out. In a hall next to it a group of men, naked to the waist, their arms so muscular that they looked swollen, were holding large wooden weights resembling bowling pins and swinging them in harmony to music. She recognized the national anthem: "Oh, Iran, oh land of jewels. . . ."

"Woman, this isn't for your view." A bearded man was standing right behind her, his face pinched with disapproval. She turned away from him and moved closer to the curb. Finally a taxi stopped and they got in.

"Will you take us to Hotel . . ." What was the name of the hotel she had passed in the bus on the way to Batul *khanoom*'s house?

"Do you want Baghi Hotel?" the driver asked.

"Yes, please."

In a few moments they reached the hotel. In the lobby she tried to assess it and was relieved to see families sitting on the sofa and in the armchairs and that it was decorated in a homey way, with tapestries on the walls.

She asked the clerk, "Do you have a room available for one night, for the two of us?"

"We have one left, you're lucky." He called to a teenage boy in uniform standing in a corner near a stairwell, "Mohsen, take them to room twenty-five."

The young boy came over, took Jennifer's overnight bag, and they all went up the stairs to the room. "If you need food or anything let me know and I'll get it for you from a restaurant outside."

"Darius, what do you want to eat, chicken, a salad?"

"I'm not hungry."

Jennifer ordered food for both of them anyway. She had a longing for a drink, strange since she rarely drank anything alcoholic, a glass of wine occasionally with dinner, a gin and tonic when offered one at social occasions. But of course it was out of the question, particularly for a woman, to ask for an alcoholic drink in this Islamic country.

She looked around the room. It was bare, modest but clean, and the bathroom had a shower and a tub in it.

In a few moments the porter brought up the food—grilled chicken, bread and rice and *doogh*—and arranged it on the table in the corner.

"Could you get us a taxi for seven in the morning?"

"Yes, *khanoom*," he said politely. Jennifer paid him and he left.

"Eat just a little, honey," she said to Darius. He took only one piece of chicken and she herself ate very little, having no appetite. Then she filled the tub for him, making the water rather cool, hoping it would bring down his fever. As she took his socks off she noticed Aziz had applied henna to the soles of his feet and his toenails. It made them look so strange. She knew the color wouldn't wear off for weeks.

Then she took him out of the tub quickly, unable to decide if a cool bath would only make him worse. She put her extra shirt on him since he had no other clothes than those he had been wearing. She tucked him into one of the twin beds.

It was getting dark outside. The voice of a muezzin calling people to prayers rose above the dying noises on the street.

"Are we going to pray?" Darius asked crankily.

"You don't have to."

Darius looked puzzled, but soon he closed his eyes and fell promptly to sleep.

She filled the tub again and got into it herself. She lay there a while, hoping to calm her nerves, which felt like they were on fire.

After her bath she picked up a magazine lying on the mantle, next to a Koran, and looked through it. Most of the pages were full of advertisements for local shops, doctors, hotels. The *maktab* was mentioned in it. "For the best religious training, bring your children to us," it said.

She began to wonder about Aziz's reaction when she went to the *maktab* and found she had taken Darius away. Dismayed, angry. It would serve her right. She couldn't forgive Aziz for what she had done.

She was very tired. She went to the window and pulled down the shade. One of the panes was broken and covered by brown paper. She went to bed in her underwear.

"Mommy," Darius called, his voice heavy with sleep. "Are you there?"

"Yes, dear, I'm here in bed, right next to you." She reached over and, finding Darius's hand, squeezed it.

Darius fell asleep again. Jennifer tried to imagine them back home, in their own beds. But in this hot little hotel room, in this ancient town, her other life seemed frighteningly unreachable. She fell into a twilight state. She heard a knock on the door and then another. Her whole body stiffened. Could it be the *pasdars?* But how would they track me down here? Still, panic-stricken, she pulled the sheet tightly around her. There was more rapping, then footsteps receding.

Chapter 22

Jennifer and Darius did not reach Teheran until two o'clock because of a long delay on the bus. They went to a small restaurant next to the bus station and ordered food and drinks. When they were finished she thought she would go to Aziz's house first so Darius and she herself could wash up and change before going to the doctor's office.

When they got to the house the door was locked. She rang the bell several times but there was no answer. She wondered if the electricity had gone out. She knocked on the door, but again no one responded. Where could everyone have gone? It was so rare for all of them to be away from the house that she didn't even have a key. She felt like smashing something. She knocked at the house next door where Azar's friend Latifeh lived. Latifeh opened the door.

"I tried to get into the house but no one answered and I don't have the key. I wondered what happened to everyone."

"You don't know? There's been an accident. A telegram came just this morning. Monir *khanoom* took Azar and Zohreh and left for Babolsar, where the men are staying. It sounded like there was only some damage to the car, nothing too serious."

"I hope that's all it is," Jennifer said, thinking about how one disaster followed another. "Do you by chance have a key to the house?"

Latifeh shook her head.

"Do you know if they're coming back tonight?"

"I doubt it, they left at noon."

"Is there any way I could get in? Do you know of a locksmith nearby?"

"No locksmith would unlock a door without the owner's permission. Once when I locked myself out, they wouldn't make a new key for me without my mother's consent, even though I live here. But you're welcome to stay with us."

There was a shout from the inside. "Latifeh, Latifeh, what's taking you so long, you've left me in the middle of . . . God break your legs for walking away from me."

"I'm sorry I took you away," Jennifer stammered.

Latifeh was blushing. "My mother just doesn't like me to leave her side for even a moment."

"Mommy, Grandma said if we pray all the time everything will be OK," Darius said as they walked away.

Jennifer didn't reply.

She was surprised to find Bijan Daneshpoor alone in the reception room with no sign of patients, no nurse or receptionist.

"Oh, it's you!" he said, looking surprised. "It's my day off.

I came back to get something." He didn't have his white jacket on, and the top buttons of his shirt were open.

It occurred to her that there was a physical resemblance between him and Karim—the broad shoulders, the hair on the chest, the closely cropped beard, something about their eyes, although the doctor seemed a few years younger than Karim.

"How is he, any better?" the doctor asked, looking at Darius.

"I'm afraid not. He still has fever. The penicillin doesn't cut it out completely though it does help to bring it down." Darius was leaning his head on her shoulder and was looking at the fish gliding in and out of a tangle of weeds in the tank.

"Did he take it all?"

"I'm not sure. He was away from me for a night, with his grandmother in Qom."

"What were they doing in Qom?"

Jennifer wasn't sure if she should talk in front of Darius. But then, in desperate need to pour out her problems, she said, "His grandmother took him there without my permission, so that they could pray at the shrine for his recovery."

"Oh, that kind of superstition. Sounds like what my mother would have done!" He added, more pensively, "The test for the strep was negative. I should take a blood sample in case of malaria or hepatitis. Since the war, with stagnant, contaminated water collected in demolished buildings, we've seen a few cases of both. But don't worry, I doubt if it's either of those or his fever would be much higher. But still it's good to be cautious." He proceeded to take a blood sample from

Darius's arm.

Darius began to cry.

"Poor little boy," Jennifer said, tears gathering in her own eyes.

The doctor put a Band-Aid on his arm and said, "Finished."

Then he labeled the sample.

Jennifer rolled down Darius's sleeve and he wandered to the fish tank.

"When I went to pick him up from his grandmother's I got arrested by a group of *pasdars*," Jennifer told the doctor.

"You're serious? What for?"

"My hair was showing, then when they found out I was an American, they became suspicious." Her voice cracked. "I escaped." She still could not shake off her fear. She imagined them speculating where she might be, how she had escaped, cursing under their breath, blaming the woman who had accompanied her to the bathroom, searching for her everywhere.

"Escaped? Amazing. How?"

"Through the bathroom window of a mosque, where they took me to wait for an ayatollah. I still can't believe I got away."

"You're really lucky. You're in a country that views America as its enemy, the source of all its problems. There's some truth to that. . . . I'm sorry, I don't mean to upset you. You were so brave to come to Iran to begin with in these turbulent times."

"No, no, it isn't that. I just have no place to stay tonight," she said, panic attacking her. She thought of Latifeh's offer but she had her invalid mother to worry about.

"You don't have a place to stay?"

"Everyone has gone somewhere and I don't have a key to the house. My husband and his uncle went on a trip and now their car has been wrecked." She could not help adding, "if that's all it is."

"It hasn't been easy for you here," he said, patting her arm sympathetically. "Why don't you come to my house instead of a hotel? It's safer, for one thing, and cheaper."

He said this naturally as if there were nothing unusual about it.

"I couldn't . . ."

"Why not? You and your son can have a room and your own private bath. I have a big house all to myself and a live-in servant."

"You've been so kind. By the way, they gave me exit visas promptly because of your letter."

"Connections are everything here. I happen to know Mobarek, who's in charge of giving exit visas."

"So it was your signature on the letter that did it."

"Shall we go to my house now?"

Her resistance was breaking down. She could not face looking for a hotel. The thought of it made her feel vulnerable, desolate. Anyway she wanted to stay as close to this doctor as possible because of Darius.

Bijan gave her a jar filled with round pills and a cup of water from the sink. "Give one to him now, one tonight, and one in the morning, and continue until we know the result of the test. It's chloroquine, in case he has malaria. It won't harm him if it turns out to be something else. We don't have a satisfactory medication for hepatitis as yet. Let me lock up and then we can go."

She gave Darius a pill and the water. The doctor's matter-of-fact manner made her more comfortable with the idea of spending the night at his house.

Chapter 23

Jennifer, sitting with Darius in the backseat of Bijan's car, felt rather dazed, numb. Bijan drove rapidly, keeping pace with the mad rush of the early evening traffic.

After about half an hour of driving, he pointed to a house. "Here we are."

The house was set in a garden, on a narrow, cobblestoned street with a view of the Alburz Mountains. He unlatched the gate and drove inside. Water was flowing from a fountain into a blue-tiled pool in the center of the garden. The air was filled with a sweet fragrance from blossoming trees and shrubs. He picked up her overnight bag and led the way onto a veranda and then a bedroom. "You and your son can sleep here," he said, putting down the bag, and then he gave them a tour of the rest of the house.

The house's architecture reminded her of Britta's house, a mixture of traditional and modern—columns on the porch, latticed windows, along with an American-style kitchen and bathrooms. Pottery and other decorative objects lay everywhere—a pair of blue Mexican candleholders, a small jade lion. "I used to do a lot of traveling, when it was easy." He pointed to the jade lion. "I brought that back from Japan."

Bijan's unpretentious, casual manner and way of dressing had not prepared her for this luxurious house. Anyway, it was too large for a single man. In a strange way it made her feel uneasy with him. What am I doing here? The question passed through her mind as if she had been brought there blindfolded.

"How about a drink first before my servant has dinner ready? Vodka, wine, apple juice, *doogh?*"

"I could really use a glass of wine," Jennifer said. She turned to Darius, "Do you want some apple juice?"

"No," he said stiffly. He was sitting close to Jennifer, with his head resting on her lap, looking glum.

Bijan left and came back in a few moments with a glass of apple juice and two glasses of wine and put them on the table before them. "I brought you apple juice anyway," he said to Darius. "Won't you have some?"

Darius took a peek at him and then hid his face on his mother's lap.

"I make my own wine," Bijan said. "I experiment with different grapes. This is with a white grape from Khasvin."

Jennifer picked up a glass and took a few sips. It had a fragrant, mellow taste. "I didn't think homemade wines could be this good." Darius yawned and rubbed his eyes. "I'd better get him ready for bed," she said. "Is there any harm giving him a bath?"

"Not as long as he doesn't have high fever."

It was a good thing to have a doctor near at hand, she thought.

As she ran the water into the tub, she caught her own reflection in the mirror, sunken cheeks, tired eyes. Her clothes were all creased. She suddenly was embarrassed to have been seen like this by the doctor, although he had acted as if everything about her was acceptable, even exciting.

Darius was very quiet as she gave him a bath. Was he frightened, puzzled, sinking into further confusion, or just too sick to care? After the bath she put her spare shirt on him again and tucked him into bed. She began to tell him a story from one of his favorite books. "Once upon a time there were three goats. . . . They wanted to get to the other side of the stream, where the grass was greener." She was halfway through when Darius fell asleep. She took a quick shower herself.

When she returned to the living room the table in the corner was set. Bijan said, "We can eat now."

They sat down on opposite sides of the table. "More wine?" he asked.

"Yes, please." Her stomach still felt tight.

He filled both her glass and his own.

She took a few quick sips of her wine, hoping it would calm her. Through the windows she could see the afterglow of the sunset fading. A few stars and the moon were faintly visible. The white muslin curtains were billowing gently in the breeze.

He put rice and *koresh* on her plate and on his own. "Please take whatever else you like."

He pointed to a photograph on the wall. "That's my family. My mother, father, sister, and me when I was twenty or so, in college. The rest are cousins and nieces. They come here a lot, they fill up all the beds."

In the picture he looked a lot like he did now, only he was thinner, his hair cut shorter, combed back more neatly.

"I never got along with my father while he was alive but after he died everything changed. When I looked at him in the casket he opened his eyes—that's really what I thought happened—and there was forgiveness there."

The strangeness of what he said made her smile.

"You think that's funny? It felt that way; the feeling is what matters."

"I see what you mean," she said, thinking she might have offended him.

"I had a very strong bond with my mother. It was because of her that I came back here from America. I had a phone call from my cousin that my mother was ill and if I didn't return I might never see her again. It made me go almost crazy. After we hung up I just sat by the phone, paralyzed. I was in my last year of medical school and couldn't even miss a day without serious consequences but as I sat there I realized my mother was more important to me than passing my exams. My mother died a year after my coming home. I got my degree from Washington University anyway though I finished up my last semester's course work in Iran."

"Then you just stayed on?"

"It's home after all."

"Have you ever been married?"

He shook his head. "There's a lot in this culture I can't accept, an arranged marriage is one of them." He seemed a bit shy and inhibited with her now, different from the way he had been in the office, as if he were not sure how to act with her. "I hoped to meet someone on my own when I was studying in America. I had a girlfriend for a while but it didn't work out."

"What went wrong?"

"I don't know," he said, looking puzzled as if he hadn't solved the mystery himself.

"Lately things have been strained between my husband and me. . . . It started with the hostage crisis, the way Iranians were treated in America. He just wasn't happy there any more and that began to take its toll on our relationship." Rebelling against confiding in this stranger, she said, "Of course I still love him." She noticed a little color coming into his face. She felt caught in a web of tangled urges, tangled emotions.

"Would you like some dessert?"

"Nothing else."

"Why don't we leave the table? Hassan will clean up later."

She went over to the sofa while he went to the phonograph to put on a record. "I'll play it on low so it won't wake Darius," he said. "Would you like to hear American or Persian music?"

"Persian," she said, partly to please him but also because that music with its soft, melancholy cadences, suited her mood right now.

He adjusted the volume a few times until it was low and yet audible enough and then he came and sat next to her. Gradually, he moved, inch by inch, closer to her, so that their arms were touching. She could smell his cologne, or was it soap? He grasped her hand and held it. She did not resist, though it made her miserable to be here with this man she hardly knew. After a moment she said, "I'd better get to bed. I'm really exhausted."

He let go of her hand. They both got up and he walked her to her room. They stood outside the door and looked at each other in the dim light. He was very attractive, she thought, with his maroon shirt casting a healthy color on his face and his curls of dark hair over his forehead. He leaned toward her and murmured like an adolescent boy, "Can I kiss you?" Not waiting for her answer, he pulled her to him and kissed her lips.

She could again smell the scent on his skin, was aware of how attractive he was, was grateful for his help, yet it all felt rather abstract. She put her hand on his arm. "I can't . . ." she said.

"I know you must be tired," he said, pulling back.

"I'm sorry."

"Good night."

"Good night."

In the room she looked at Darius. He was breathing deeply, rhythmically. She got undressed and lay on the bed in her underwear again. Moths were beating against the window. Cicadas carried on in the trees. She clutched the pillow and shut her eyes.

She woke to the crowing of a rooster somewhere and the hum of traffic. Sunlight was pouring into the room. She remembered immediately where she was. She rose on her elbow and checked on Darius. He was still asleep. She got dressed and went into the living room. Bijan wasn't there. Her eyes caught a folded sheet of paper on the dining table, with Jennifer written on it. She picked it up and opened it. "Jennifer, I thought I would let you sleep. I had to go to work but I'll be back early this afternoon. By then I should have the result of Darius's test." The servant came in, carrying breakfast on a tray, and began to arrange it on the table. Bread, cheese, butter, jam, fruit, tea. He was very small and had a brooding, sly manner. He did not show the slightest surprise at her presence. She sat down and had bread and butter and tea. Forced herself to.

Chapter 24

Karim's briefcase had not turned up at the police station, when he checked with them. It seemed he had no choice but to apply for a new passport in Teheran. What was going to happen if he could not get one quickly? Darius's school would be starting in September, so would his teaching, and there was Jennifer's work.

He began to walk through the town, studying its structure. He came across an old *karvansary* with a sign saying, "Under reconstruction." He found a back door open and went in. The building was tilting slightly as if it were about to collapse. The rooms, off a columned porch, were ornamented with engravings and friezes of animals and flowers. One wall was covered by a faded tapestry of a man and woman sitting under a willow tree, each holding a glass of wine, another depicted men on horses moving through clouds. He could imagine travelers, usually alone, usually male, having stopped here overnight on the way to a distant destination. Sometimes they would get a *sigheh* for the night as he and his uncle had. He looked closely at the half-demolished, repainted entrance door, and he scratched off some of the paint with a key. An intricate arabesque design of flowers and animals were revealed underneath.

Then he sat on a bench on the porch, contemplating how he would restore the place. As he sat there he had a vivid image of himself as a voyager through life—first in Iran, then America, now back in Iran.

He left the *karvansary* to get some food before everything closed for the afternoon siesta. He sat on the terrace of a restaurant, overlooking the sea. The roof of the terrace consisted of a thickly woven layer of grape leaves, interspersed with jasmine flowers. He ate while watching the boats gliding on the water and children playing on the sand. The sight of the children made him miss Darius terribly. He wondered again about the consequences for all of them if they were late getting back home to the States. But the idea of going back to the same job, the same town, depressed him. The conversations he had had with the neighbors about a broken lawn mower or how to mend a patch of grass, and in the winter, when the landscape turned cold and barren, about the best way to melt ice in the driveway, seemed unconnected to him and unreal. That wasn't really him. It was just a posture he had put on, for too long, it seemed.

The same neighbors with whom he thought he had good relationships had begun to say incredible, unfair things. "We have nothing against you personally, but are those fanatics from Iran going to murder any more people all over the world?" They spoke the word Iran with such disdain, as if it were the worst hellhole, populated by murderers.

He took out a photograph of Darius, Jennifer, and himself from his wallet. It was taken a year ago in the backyard of their house in Athens. How deceptive it was; it reflected none of the turmoil that had been simmering under the surface of their lives then. Hadn't Nancy, who took the picture, said several times, "Smile," or, "Relax, you're looking stiff." Nancy herself was always cheerful, even when things weren't going well for her. Come to think of it, it seemed he really didn't know Nancy or Don, their true feelings and thoughts about things. They had a facade that stood like a wall between them and others.

He could not stop the flow of negative memories. That day when he had gone to see Ed in his office to talk about his promotion. He had thought he could make a good case for himself; his recent publications were being cited more frequently than anyone else's in the department. Ed handed a batch of papers to him; they were student evaluations of him as a teacher that Ed must have kept in a file. Karim had been given copies of them at the time and already knew what the students thought of him. Most of the comments were favorable; only a few thought he needed to give more structure to the class.

"I've already read these," Karim said.

Ed said through pursed lips, without looking at him, "I want you to look at them again—in light of promotion. Did you notice the specifics, lack of structure, lack of clarity?"

"Well, do *you* have trouble understanding me?"

"Sometimes," Ed said. "Look, I'll put you up next year.

Meanwhile work on your teaching and get a few more articles out."

There was clearly no reasoning with this man, Karim had thought. Of course Ed himself was trapped in a situation he hated, but was that enough to excuse him? It was common knowledge that his grant applications had been repeatedly rejected; his research was terrible; his wife had left him for someone in the arts department. His attempts to establish relationships with new women had not worked out. He viewed his two sons as failures—it was rumored that one was heavily involved in drugs, the other had been put in a mental hospital twice for "aggressive behavior." A sense of failure, of being trapped, in fact permeated the whole department. He tried to recall the good aspects of his life in Athens—the serenity of their house, for instance, the pleasure of riding his bicycle on quiet streets back and forth to school, the cool fresh air in the morning as he and Jennifer hiked near their house; but no comfort came to him. Instead, looking back, those scenes seemed like picture postcards, beautiful, but flat and distant.

He left the restaurant and went into a small park. For an instant he was transfixed by the sight of a woman sitting on a bench. She was following the dress code only loosely—wearing her *chador* so that much of her hair was revealed, and she had light makeup on. He couldn't take his eyes off her. She looked a little like Soroor, the prostitute he had spent that night with—and of Jhaleh, the girl from long ago. The woman turned around and their eyes locked in a mutual, curious stare. A flame leapt up inside him under her gaze. Then she got up and walked away. He was tempted to follow her, ask her questions, but managed to restrain himself.

When he and Fereidoon got to the hospital the nurse told Karim his uncle was doing very well and could be taken home. Then she gave him a prescription. "I hope you'll be able to fill this. There's a shortage of heart medicine . . . He'll have to rest as much as possible and avoid eating too much fat or eggs. And absolutely no cigarettes."

"Would he be able to take a car ride back to Teheran?"

"As long as he isn't driving." She guided them to Jamshid's room.

Jamshid was dressed and waiting for them. He looked well, his color was good. He had already taken care of the small bill, he said. "Most of the costs are paid for by the government. In spite of the war, we still have good health care in Iran."

At the house, they took Jamshid into a room they had prepared for him—Fereidoon had put a radio next to the bed and a pot full of geraniums in a corner.

They sat with Jamshid for a few moments and then left him to rest.

Chapter 25

After breakfast Jennifer left with Darius for Aziz's house to see if anyone was home, but again the door was locked and no one was there.

Darius was suddenly full of questions. Why can't we get into the house? Where is grandma now? When is daddy coming back? Why are we staying at the doctor's house? Jennifer tried to answer everything in a way that would not upset him.

How serious was the accident? She was worned about Karim; yet she couldn't shake off her anger at him. She decided to go to Turkish Airlines to see if she could change the tickets to an earlier date—she had their passports and tickets in her purse. At the airline office an agent checked his computer and found a flight to Istanbul on Thursday, four days later.

"Nothing earlier?"

The man shook his head. She gave him the tickets and he reissued new ones for them.

She paused on the street wondering what to do—check

into a hotel and keep checking at the house to see if anyone was back?

It seemed best just to go back to Bijan's house at least tonight. On the way back she bought a few necessities for Darius and herself—underwear, a T-shirt, and pants.

When they got back, the servant was standing by the gate, looking up and down the street in a vigilant way.

"*Khanoom*, I'm glad you're back. The doctor called. He said he wouldn't have advised you to go out," he said in his heavy, ponderous way, not looking at her. "He gave me instructions to do all your errands for you."

"Don't worry about it," she said, trying to seem nonchalant. "This was something I had to take care of myself."

Above the roar of the traffic outside she heard a demonstration starting somewhere, faraway voices of a mob shouting. It began to recede and finally it faded.

"I know America will yield, and become an Islamic Republic," the servant said.

She was startled by the concept but also by the fact that he was acknowledging he knew she was an American.

In a few moments he served them lunch. She and Darius ate and then she took him into their room and put him down for a nap. His temperature was a little above normal; his fever came and went mysteriously. Hassan had put two glasses, a carafe with ice in it, and a bottle of mosquito repellent on the table. He had also brought a portable fan to supplement the slow-moving one on the ceiling. Through the window she could see two herons in a nest, only their heads visible. Tiny yellow butterflies fluttered around the flowers. The air here was cleaner, freer from smog, than where Aziz lived, making the sunlight, the sky, purer in color. The place was enchanting, magical, now in bright daylight—too bad that Darius was sick, that the circumstances of her being here were so strange.

Bijan returned at four, holding a package and a sleek red toy sports car. "The car is for Darius," he said.

"Oh, he's going to really like it."

"I got the result of the blood tests, he doesn't have malaria or hepatitis."

"What could it be then?" Anxiety shot up in her.

"Some kind of bacteria or virus, but it can't be too serious."

"We went to see if anyone was home but the door was still locked."

"I was hoping you'd stay on here."

"We'll be leaving for the United States on Thursday."

"Too bad, just as we're getting to know each other. Are you sure you want to leave so soon?" He looked visibly disappointed.

He gave her the package. "I bought some clothes for you and Darius. I guessed at the sizes. I hope they fit."

"You're doing so much for us."

He suddenly leaned over and kissed her on her lips, first gently and then more forcefully.

"I'm a married woman," she whispered.

"You left your husband when you came with me to my house, it amounts to that."

It does feel like I have left Karim, she thought. This is something he would never forgive me for if he knew about it. They embraced, kissing for a few moments. The ceiling fan was whirring slowly. She pulled back as Darius wandered into the room.

Bijan gave him the red car. Darius took it reluctantly.

"Do you want to play a card game with me? No? Then I can do some tricks for you," Bijan said to him.

Darius was unresponsive, but Bijan got a pack of cards. He sat down and said to Darius, "Take a card, now put it back in the deck." Then Bijan shuffled the deck and pulled out the card. "This is the one?" he asked.

"Yes," Darius said, a faint smile coming into his face.

Bijan did another trick and another one, talking to Darius in English and Farsi, back and forth. He finally stopped when Darius began to look tired and leaned his head on Jennifer's shoulder.

"We'll try the clothes on." She took Darius into their room and pulled out the clothes from the box one by one—for her a yellow cotton blouse with dark blue rectangles painted on it, an off-white skirt, a pink nightgown, and for Darius; a navy blue dress, two pairs of jeans and two T-shirts. She helped him try them on. They fit perfectly. She tried on the skirt and blouse and then the dress. They were slightly big, half a size or so, but they looked good enough. Something about the blouse was making her sad. It was that day. . . . She and Karim were walking past some shops in Columbus. Karim pointed to a yellow dress with dark blue floral designs that was displayed in a shop window. "Perfect for you, with your coloring," he had said, and they had gone in for her to try it on. She had worn that dress for several years. How could this have happened to us? Many of their friends who had problems in their marriages sought out affairs, but she never thought that would be something she would do. She thought of the wife of one of the men in her company who left him for their young baby-sitter. It had been a scandal. "She left him for another woman?" people asked. Then they had started speculating, "Would you mind it more if your spouse left you for someone the same sex or the opposite sex?" She wondered now if Karim would mind it more or less if she slept with someone from his own country. An odd comparison. She was struck again by the impossibility of their situation. He was unhappy in the United States and she would be unhappy living in Iran. At the beginning when she married Karim she had been delighted to immerse herself in his culture, but now in Iran it was as if she were impersonating someone else, just being here, conforming to the rules. And Karim had never become a true American, or his sense of identity could not be so easily threatened in a crisis. She *felt* for the first time, what before she had only understood in a cerebral way, what Karim had been through in a culture alien to him in so many ways. Tears rolled down her cheeks. She sat at the edge of the bed and breathed deeply a few times, trying to calm herself.

Chapter 26

"Why don't we have dinner at a restaurant," Bijan suggested. "I'll be careful, so no one will see us."

It was after dusk when they got into his car and he drove away from the city. Even in the dark, Jennifer was keenly aware of every face she saw on the streets, in other cars.

In a short while they were at the outskirts of the city. They passed a caved-in structure that must have been a part of the foundation of a building, huge machines lying on the road, abandoned.

"They were starting to build high-rises here, under the shah," Bijan explained. "The shah had the grandiose ambition of making Iran the Switzerland of the East. Now we're back to being a Third-World country again. Our economy is shattered, the machinery he acquired is all abandoned and rusting. But in most ways things are better now for the masses of our people. Each neighborhood has a mullah to give the people advice on their problems in accord with Islam—what to do with a wayward daughter, how to put up with financial difficulties, domestic disputes. Also they raise money for the poor, a servant who loses his job, a man who can't work because of some disability."

"What about the oppression of women, of people of different religions, and the censorship, the anti-intellectualism?"

"Yes, you're right, a lot of bad things. More repressiveness in certain areas, but there was something degrading about being an Iranian under the shah. Now at least we don't have to pretend we're more Western than Westerners themselves." He turned the car into a small alley and parked in front of a restaurant.

They sat outdoors in a dark corner of the restaurant garden. In a moment the waiter brought over scallions, radishes, cheese, and a flat bread and put them on the table, then he took their orders. The menu had the usual selections, kebabs, chicken or lamb, *koresh*, *khuku*, yogurt and cucumber salad, and *doogh* to drink. Jennifer ordered chicken kebabs for her and Darius and Bijan had the ground lamb kebab. Bijan told the waiter to bring salads and *doogh* for everyone. The waiter asked if they wanted raw eggs with their rice. They all said no. When he brought their food he also had ground sumac for the meat and lumps of butter for the rice. Darius, after eating a little, went to the pool to watch the colorful water, green, yellow, and blue, flowing into it from a fountain.

"See how easily we pass as a family," Bijan said.

She was silent for a moment. Then she said, "I shouldn't have ordered anything, I'm not hungry."

"What's the matter, do you have an upset stomach?"

She couldn't help herself, she said, "I'm dying to go back home."

"I wish you wouldn't talk like that, there's so much that you haven't seen yet that I can introduce you to. You could stay with me in my house, I want you there. No one will find out if we're careful."

"You don't really think it would work, do you?"

"We could make it work."

"Some of the best things have to end," she said after a moment. "Because they're impractical."

"You sound so American."

Darius came back and climbed onto her lap. In a few moments he fell asleep. He slept through the performance of a group of musicians who came onto the platform next to the pool and began to play drums, cymbals, and violins.

Jennifer could hear Bijan's and her own voices, sounding sad and romantic as they filtered through the music.

Darius was sweating as he slept in her arms, though a breeze had begun to blow. "Shall we go back?" she asked.

Darius slept the whole time on the car ride back. At home she sat on her bed and cried again, overwhelmed by confusion, helplessness. After a while she managed to pull herself together and she went into the living room, where Bijan was sipping a glass of wine.

He poured her a glass too and they sat together, kissing. In a few moments he took her hand and led her into his bedroom. In bed he helped her undress and then he took his own clothes off. They talked and touched, talked and touched. She was aware of a quickening in her heart, a thrill at the newness of his body. Their bodies became plastered together with sweat and semen. Finally they lay back.

"You know Jennifer, I'm falling in love with you," he said.

"You don't know me."

"I know you well, you've always been with me."

His intensity both drew and upset her. It was like drinking a sweet but poisonous substance. Nothing felt quite real.

"I won't let you go back. It will work out. I have money, connections." Then he said, dreamily, "I'll get anything you want and bring it home, we'll hire a tutor for Darius and we'll leave the house only at night, we'll take long trips."

She laughed. "It sounds like a fairy tale."

"You could make it real."

"I have to get back to my life."

"I won't let you!"

After a while she fell asleep, and when she opened her eyes again she could see through the slats in the blinds that the sky was getting light. Bijan was still asleep, one of his hands resting on her thigh, his face serene. She removed his hand gently and got out of the bed. She wrapped her blouse around her and, picking up the rest of her clothes, tiptoed out and went to her room.

"Mommy, climb up here with me," Darius said.

"What did you say?" Darius did not answer. Obviously he had been talking in his sleep.

In the morning Bijan had left early again before she had awakened. She wondered if she should go to Aziz's house to see if anyone was back, and then decided not to. She couldn't face anyone now, after having slept with Bijan. All she wanted to do was to leave the country and deal with the consequences later.

Darius wandered through the rooms, went out into the garden and back, lost and aimless. Jennifer told him the names of some of the flowers—morning glory, violet. Then Hassan gave him seeds to feed to the pigeons, but he seemed tired and soon went to his room and lay down.

She looked through the bookshelves on the living room walls, trying to find something to read, but they were filled with medical books and journals. She took out a journal and began to read some of the articles—malaria was a big problem in Iranian villages, stomach cancer was common among Iranian women. She shut the journal, it was only making her anxious.

She turned on the television and began to watch it mindlessly. A devout young virgin, sixteen years old, was about to martyr herself by becoming a "Bride of Blood." She was going to Lebanon to drive a car full of dynamite into an American military unit. Her reward, she was told, was that she would go to heaven and, once there, a husband, more devout than could be found on this earth, and very handsome and gentle, would be selected for her. She wore a kerchief and a long-sleeved dress with a skirt that came down to her ankles. In spite of her suicidal mission her face was radiant, her eyes were filled with excitement. It was terrible, horrifying to watch the destructiveness of such devotion. The program was coming to a close.

The woman, now wearing a frilly white wedding gown, glittering jewelry, and a wreath of flowers on her head, was holding hands with a handsome young man in a dark suit. They were slowly floating upward through fluffy clouds in the sky.

Chapter 27

Jennifer sat in the living room and sketched designs on paper she had found stacked by the phone. It calmed her somewhat to be working. She thought of a pattern of blue and green swirling lines, the color of the mosaic used frequently here in decoration. It would look good on a thin, silk fabric.

There was a loud knock on the outside door. She listened intently, on edge. She went to the window to see who it was. A young woman, wearing a blue *roopush* with her hair covered by a scarf, appeared in the garden.

"Is Dr. Daneshpoor in?" the woman asked, taken aback by finding her there.

"He's away at work."

"Are you Bijan's new . . . ?"

"He's just . . ." Her voice faltered. Then she went on more firmly, ". . . helping my son and me. You can wait for him if you like."

The woman came inside and sat down on a chair. She took off her scarf and let her long, deep chestnut hair flow over her shoulders. Her eyes were the same color as her hair. She was very pretty and young, no more than twenty-one or twenty-two. "My name is Fereshdeh," she said.

"Jennifer."

"You're an American, but you know Farsi so well."

"I'm married to an Iranian."

Fereshdeh's eyes were riveted on her with curiosity. "Really?"

"My son and I have had some complications. Bijan has been very kind to help us out."

Fereshdeh kept staring at her, waiting for her to elaborate, it seemed. Then she said, "I saw the dress you're wearing somewhere. Yes, in the window of Naiin Shop."

Jennifer felt herself blushing. She was wearing the dress that Bijan had bought for her.

"Didn't he mention me to you?" the woman asked.

"No. But I haven't been here that long."

Fereshdeh looked very upset now as she picked up her purse and took out an envelope from inside it. "This is a letter from him. I brought it to remind him of his promises." She handed it to Jennifer.

Jennifer began to read it.

> My dear Fereshdeh,
> How can I tell you what a difference knowing you has made? You're like a life-saving potion. Before meeting you I thought of death all the time; existence was meaningless. When will I have you to myself? When will I share my life with you . . .

She stopped reading. The date on it, she noticed, was in April. Why is it I feel so betrayed by this man to whom I have no real claim, she thought, a man I've known only for a few days? But her heart was thudding unpleasantly.

"He practically kept me a prisoner for two years," the woman said, keeping her eyes steadily on Jennifer. "Now he doesn't know me." She took the letter back and got up restlessly. "I'm going to his office." Then with an air of pride she added, "Don't misunderstand, I'm not going to beg him to take me back, I just want him to talk to me about it in a respectful way like he used to." She walked away with languorous steps. She paused by the door and said, "I'm sorry to have disturbed you."

Jennifer watched her go through the garden, passing the servant who was pulling weeds from a flower bed, his face hidden behind a straw hat.

Bijan returned around four o'clock. He took out a little box from his briefcase and gave it to her. "A present for you."

"Another present? You're spoiling me."

She opened the box and found a gold ring set with sapphire stones clustered together on it to form a flower. "This is beautiful, but how can I? No, I can't accept this . . ." Apprehension swept over her. His lavish presents and attention, his insistence that she stay on, his words, "I won't let you," all had a threatening undertone. What if he tried to hold her back somehow?

"You've filled my days with pleasure," he said, taking the ring from her and trying it on different fingers. It fit her middle left hand finger perfectly.

She looked at it next to her braided wedding band. The juxtaposition filled her, more than anything else, with a sense of loss.

"Anyway I have no one to spend my money on," he said, half-joking.

She wondered if she should bring up the young woman. After a moment of hesitation, she said, "Someone came here to see you. . . ."

"Yes, I know, Fereshdeh. She came to my office. I hope she didn't bother you too much." A flicker of embarrassment passed over his face. His voice was dismissive as he said, "I must admit I was carried away by her once. Then reality hit me—that she and her family were only after my prestige and wealth. I would only be a symbol to them."

"Aren't I a symbol to you too. My being an American?" For a moment it was as if she were playing a dizzy game whose rules she didn't quite understand herself.

He laughed. "But a more worthy one. You represent a free, independent woman."

"I wouldn't be so free living here."

As if he had not heard her, following his own train of thought, he said, "When I was just a small boy I used to play house with little girls, my cousins mainly—I played the father or the doctor—I always imagined my playmate, no matter what she looked like in reality, to have blue eyes and curly blond hair, like the foreign dolls I'd seen on display in shop windows. They looked like you."

She tried to hide her feelings of apprehension. She said,

"It's odd, but I too always had foreign looking boys in my fantasies."

"We're a good match then," he said, smiling. He leaned over and kissed her hard on the lips. "You do believe me, don't you, that I'm in love with you?"

"If that's possible after three days!"

"Oh, Jennifer, don't be so skeptical, tell me how do you feel about me?"

"I'm attracted to you, of course . . ."

"That's all, attracted?"

"I'm leaving in two days."

"You will change your mind."

She was relieved when Darius came into the room, interrupting them.

Chapter 28

Patches of light were gleaming in the distance as Karim and Jamshid approached Teheran. Monir, Azar, and Zohreh, who had turned up unexpectedly in Babolsar, had remained behind to take the bus in the morning, so that there would be room in the car for Jamshid to lie down in the backseat.

In Teheran the streets were relatively free of traffic at that late hour of the night and they drove through the city quickly. Some tea houses were open and men were sitting in the dim interiors or on platforms outside, smoking waterpipes and talking. Jamali Avenue was quiet. Gas lamps blinked in the windows of the Meli bank. Karim parked in the garage, next to the bank, where his uncle kept the car, and helped him out.

At the house Jamshid opened the door with his key. Karim saw him to his room, then went into his own.

He was surprised that Jennifer and Darius weren't there. Then he remembered Monir had said something about them having gone to Qom with Aziz. He noticed an airmail letter on his bed. He picked it up and looked at the sender's address.

It was from Nancy Carpenter. He opened it, though it was addressed to Jennifer, and looked through it quickly.

> Dear Jennifer,
>
> We're eagerly waiting for some news from you. Your house is all in order. Joe has been mowing the lawn regularly. I've watered the plants—the azaleas though are finally dying—and I've been bringing your mail inside. I didn't see anything urgent enough to mail to you, but anyway you may be back here before it would get to you. A good play series is starting on the campus. We should try to take advantage of it this year...

The rest seemed to be gossip about other women she and Jennifer knew. He stopped reading. It was paradoxical how the very things that had drawn him to the American way of life were now depressing him.

He got into his pajamas and went to bed. The street lamp behind the window cast a yellow light into the room. Moths clung to the lamp like bits of paper. The alley had remained so much the same. Even the telephone poles seemed to have the same birds sitting on them as in his childhood.

Voices of boys talking and laughing reached him from the alley. One of them began to whistle softly the tune to a song Karim knew well. "I'm only fourteen, full of dreams. Bright dreams like stars against a black sky." He thought of himself at that age. He had been studious, made friends with boys who dreamed of changing things for the better, thin, idealistic boys, full of philosophical questions and ideas. But now he felt exhilarated just being in this familiar house, city, surrounded by the sights and sounds of his youth.

What is a realistic solution for us? he wondered. Maybe they could live in Iran part of the year and in the United States the other part. It would be hard to balance it out fairly. The whistling outside stopped suddenly and so did the voices . . .

Karim looked at the clock on the mantle. It was already eleven. He'd slept very late. From the window he could see bits of clouds reflected in the *joob*.

He heard his mother saying to someone in the courtyard, "She took him and ran away without telling me."

"She's used to a different life," the other woman said.

He put his clothes on quickly, and went into the courtyard. Aziz was sitting on the rug with Latifeh, who seemed to have just dropped in—she still had her chador on.

"Jennifer came to Qom and took Darius away," Aziz said as soon as she saw him. She looked worn, dust had settled on her dark dress and on her chador which lay rumpled around her; a suitcase stood next to her on the rug.

"They aren't here, I don't understand . . ."

"They aren't back?" A startled, naked look, came into Aziz's face. "I wanted to pray for my grandson at the shrine and send him to the *maktab*. I'm an old woman, I don't understand what goes on in the world. I sit home most of the time and read the Koran and pray. I'm doing the best I can until God takes me away."

"Where could they be?" Karim mumbled. "They have no friends here."

"She and Darius came to my house when they couldn't get in," Latifeh said.

"When was that?"

"The day before yesterday, or maybe it was the day before that. I asked her to stay in my house but she didn't accept."

"She's taken my grandson away," Aziz said, lamenting, and she began to cry. She hit herself on the head with the palms of her hands.

Karim wandered outside and looked up and down the street.

It was as if he had been thrown into a dark body of water, was lost in it, not knowing what direction to move. Images rushed by his eyes, images of Jennifer in shorts and a straw hat, working on their backyard vegetable garden, of the two of them bicycling on summery green country roads, and of Darius walking around the zoo with him, looking and laughing at the animals.

He sometimes played hide-and-seek with Darius. Like a child he would hide in a closet or under the bed while Darius went about calling, "Daddy, I'm going to find you." Sometimes if it took too long for Darius to spot him, he made himself partially visible. It was such a delightful moment when Darius said, "Daddy, I found you, you're there, come out," as he reached over to grab at his sleeve or the edge of his trousers.

"Daddy, will you take me on camel rides and elephant rides in Iran?" Darius had asked him as they were packing for this trip. Karim had smiled. "If we can find any of that in Iran."

"James's mother said they have them in India."

"Iran isn't exactly like India. But there are lots of nice things in Iran we could do." He had told him he would teach him how to fly a kite, take him to a building that swayed back and forth without collapsing. Yet in Iran he had not done any of that, occupied as he was with his uncle's needs. Of course that was urgent under the circumstances, but still . . .

He walked to Jamali Avenue, and for an instant he thought he saw them in the backseat of a car and he ran to the curb. But as he looked closer he realized that the woman and the child didn't even resemble Jennifer and Darius. Where could they possibly be? Was she in trouble? Could she have left the country? He kept looking up and down the street, hoping to see them get out of a taxi or come out of a shop.

He decided to go to Turkish Airlines to find out if Jennifer had changed the tickets.

Chapter 29

The phone was ringing. Jennifer looked at her watch. It was already eight in the morning. The servant must be out somewhere. She got up, put on her bathrobe quickly, and went to answer the phone, but it had stopped ringing by the time she got to it.

Bijan was supposed to come back early today and take them to the airport. Everything made her anxious, even the anticipation of leaving made her feel as though she were on the plane just circling, unable to land.

It was hard to believe they had been in this house for such a brief time. Every day Bijan went to work and came back early; then they went out for dinner or for a ride, always after dark. Once he took her to an ancient palace, each room of which had belonged to a different wife in a shah's harem. Another evening they went to a mill and from the old tower they looked out over the expanse of the city.

He told her that anything could be obtained in Teheran, although you might have to pay a high price for it. One night he brought home a few videos of American movies and they watched *Prizzi's Honor*. Late at night she would go to his bed. He was always avid in his lovemaking, unpredictable, a little theatrical. They got very little sleep. She didn't understand how he could function at work.

The longer she stayed in Iran, the more the country confounded her. There were all the surface rules and restrictions, women covered up, no alcohol, yet decadence flourished underneath. Prostitutes furtively roamed the streets—she had seen some of them lurking in doorways when she was passing Laleh Zar Avenue, revealing naked legs under their chadors for an instant and then covering them again. A black market made almost anything, from videos to alcohol, available. With the anti-American slogans and demonstrations went a deep admiration for American ways. Children's lunch boxes, clothes, and sheets had American cartoon characters on them.

The phone started ringing again. She picked it up. "Hello."

"Hello."

Then click. The voice, from that one word, sounded like the pretty young woman who had come to the house the other day.

She got Darius out of bed and they had breakfast, and then she began to pack their belongings in a small suitcase Bijan had told her she could take. She would leave what was at Aziz's house.

How could she let them know she was going home with Darius without all sorts of questions being raised, thorny complications? It would be best to leave and send a telegram from Istanbul, where they had an eight-hour wait between flights.

Hassan came into their room, holding a pitcher of water with ice tinkling in it. "It's supposed to be hotter than ever tonight. You and the child are going to need this," he said.

"We won't be here tonight, we're leaving. Didn't the doctor tell you?"

Instead of answering he said, "It's all up to God." He put down the pitcher and left.

They still had two hours before they were to leave. Two hours. It seemed intolerably long.

She had a terrible headache. She went to her bathroom to look for aspirin but couldn't find any in the medicine cabinet, so she tried the bathroom off Bijan's bedroom. She found a bottle of them in the large cabinet there. She took two, and then, curious, she looked to see what the other bottles contained. Most of them, labeled in Farsi, had names she didn't recognize. She was surprised at the sheer number of them. She suddenly suspected that many of them were amphetamines—that would explain why Bijan was so energetic and sleepless at night. The idea somehow depressed her. Maybe it was the way he lived in general, somehow dissolute in spite of his dedication to his work.

The phone was ringing again. In a moment the servant called out to her, "*Khanoom*, it's for you, the doctor."

She went to the phone, upset. Why was he calling when he should be here by now?

"Jennifer, I'm sorry but I'm going to be a little late. I was called to the hospital. I have to go."

"Can't you . . ."

"Don't worry, I'll be back in time for you to catch your plane."

He sounded rushed and impatient, making her wonder if he really intended to come back on time at all. Last night hadn't he said again, "I can't let you go now that I've found you."

Then she thought, what's stopping me from leaving right now? Once the idea had formed in her mind it seemed the only logical thing to do. If she waited until one and Bijan still hadn't come it would be nearly impossible to depend on taxis or buses because of the afternoon siesta. She tore a piece of paper from the pad by the phone and tried to think of something to write to Bijan but her mind went blank. What could she say? Finally she jotted down, "Dear Bijan, I must rush to the airport. Thank you so much for the beautiful shelter and all that you did for us . . ." She stared at the sapphire ring on her finger, twinkling in the dimness of the corridor. She couldn't possibly keep it.

She took it off and put it with the note in an envelope she found in the table drawer. She sealed it and left it by the phone.

She put her hands on Darius's shoulders, "Honey, we're going to the airport right away."

"Are we going home?"

"Yes."

"Is Daddy coming home?"

"Yes, later."

"Does Daddy like Bijan?"

The unexpected question threw Jennifer off balance. It took her a moment to say, "I think he would."

"OK."

"Remember, it's going to be a very long trip. You have to be very patient."

"I know," Darius said, pushing his hair back over his ear, a gesture of pride. His hair was now longer than usual, dishevelled.

She picked up the small suitcase, glad that the servant was nowhere in sight. Outside they walked a few blocks until they reached the wider, busier avenue, where she hailed a taxi. The sun was shining brightly and the shadows were long, almost black. The taxi seat was hot, stinging her even through her chador. She put Darius on her lap to protect him from burning.

The traffic was heavier than she had ever seen it. Cars honked continuously, cut in front of each other. A yellow Paykan was pushing in front of their taxi. The taxi driver put his hand on the horn and kept it there, then opening the window, he began to shout, "Son of a whore, whoremonger."

Darius clutched at Jennifer's arms. Jennifer herself had gone rigid.

The driver of the Paykan suddenly jumped out of his car and came and stood in front of the taxi's window. "Are you a donkey or a human being?" Suddenly he slapped the taxi driver's face. "I'm an engineer, you're a nobody, a donkey." Then just as abruptly he dashed back into his car.

"If I didn't have a woman and a child in my backseat I'd get out and break your skull," the taxi driver shouted, his face, where he had been slapped, beet red. "You son of a whore."

Jennifer held Darius to herself tightly and kept looking at her watch. It had taken half an hour to get through fifteen blocks or so. But then the taxi driver managed to push past the yellow Paykan and entered the flow of traffic again.

They finally reached the airport. The driver asked for twice as much as it read on the meter and Jennifer paid him without resistance. Her knees were shaky as she entered the terminal.

Chapter 30

The terminal was crowded with a motley group of people lined up at different counters or sitting and waiting, their luggage piled around them—two Arab men wearing turbans, several Kurdish women and children in baggy pants and full-skirted dresses, an English-looking couple, and some others whose nationalities Jennifer could not identify. The heterogeneity was a relief, making it easier for her to blend in, but still she could not really relax.

She looked for the Turkish Airlines counter and found it in the middle of the terminal. "Passports and tickets please," the agent said. She gave him the tickets and passports.

"These haven't been stamped," the man said after looking through the passports. "Take them to that window. They'll stamp them if there are no problems with them. You were supposed to have done that two or three hours earlier."

"We have exit visas already."

"This has nothing to do with visas."

She walked away with Darius and asked him sit on a chair

and wait for her. She put the luggage next to him and dashed to the passport window.

There were a few people ahead of her. A young man with a bushy beard was in charge. Smoke rose from a half-lit cigarette in an ashtray in front of him. The couple he was helping seemed to have a million questions. Jennifer shifted from foot to foot until finally it was her turn.

"What time is your flight?" the man asked.

"In an hour."

"You should have brought your passports over earlier."

"I'm sorry, I didn't know. My child is sick, I have to take him to his own doctor," she rambled on.

"Aren't there enough doctors here?"

"Yes, of course, but I thought . . ."

"Where's your child?"

What business of his is this, she thought, but she managed to say politely, "I left him over there with the luggage."

"You left your sick child alone?"

"I'm keeping an eye on him."

The man shook his head. But then, he looked through both passports, stamped them, and gave them back.

"Thank you so much," she said, incredulous that the passports were back in her hands.

She and Darius hurried to the customs line. It was moving very slowly because of the huge amount of luggage some of the passengers had. A few of the suitcases were so full that they had to be tied with ropes.

When it was her turn, the customs inspector asked her,

"That's all you have?"

"Yes, we're traveling lightly."

"Open them." She opened the suitcase and the overnight bag, avoiding his eyes. "No rugs, no gold?"

"We have nothing."

"Go ahead, you can shut them."

They had to go behind curtains to be searched, she by women and Darius by men. The women searched her purse, her clothes, even inside her shoes.

On the phone Darius sat next to the window with a look of intense misery on his face, then he began to cry.

"What's wrong? what's the matter?"

"I miss daddy, I miss grandma," he said through tears.

"He'll come home soon and maybe your grandma will come too," she said. She took out a handkerchief from her purse and wiped his tears. The handkerchief, embroidered at the corner, was given to her by Azar in return for a nightgown. How could I be leaving like this, without saying goodbye, she thought, struck by guilt and remorse.

Several strands of conversation in different languages were going on around her. Two Iranian women sitting on the other side of the aisle were apparently going to Turkey to see if they could get visas to go to France. Two men in front of her were hoping to get visas for the United States. One of them said, "I have a letter of invitation from my son, he's a doctor in California, that should make it easier."

She began to think of their house in Athens waiting for them. Darius's room, with his stuffed animals, books, records, toys, arranged on shelves. The room she used as her study, just above the circular stairway, a photo blow-up of the three of them on her desk. In the photograph they were wearing the matching Hawaiian clothes (Karim and Darius in shirts and she in a muumuu), all in bright orange with designs of green branches, that her parents had brought back for them from a Hawaiian vacation. The red chair in the living room Karim liked to sink into late at night with a drink to watch the news or a movie on TV. He loved old movies, especially Westerns, some of which he had seen as an adolescent in Iran. They had given him his first impressions of the United States (false ones, he had said, laughing). Their backyard, planted so that in every season there was something in bloom—holly bushes bearing red berries in the winter, dogwoods full of white blossoms in spring. The patio, where they ate most of their meals when it was warm enough, the air crystalline clear so much of the time and so quiet that they could hear the slightest quivering of the trees and the jingling of the wind chimes hanging on a branch. They watched the sun rise or set as they ate. . . . But then all the underlying sadness and tension mounting, until everything turned dark for Karim, even menacing . . .

Chapter 31

The air smelled of grass mingled with a faint aroma of flowers and wood smoke as Jennifer and Darius arrived at their house in Athens. A soft moist light shone over everything.

The house was in order, plants all watered, the lawn mowed. Nancy had put their mail on the dining table. But as she walked through the house, room to room, the sight of Karim's belongings, his clothes hanging in the closet, his bathrobe on the back of a chair in the bedroom, filled her with loneliness.

Darius went immediately into his room. She could hear him talking to his stuffed animals. "I missed you," or "Don't be afraid." His temperature had vanished by the time they reached Athens, and the thin, exhausted quality had left his voice. Still, she thought she would take him to see his pediatrician.

As she unpacked the phone rang several times, but when she picked it up she couldn't hear a voice on the other end. She was sure it was Karim, trying to reach her. Then she tried to call him herself, but the lines were always busy. She set her phone on redial. No matter how many times it rang she never got through.

That night in bed she was haunted by the extraordinary beauty and the extreme harshness, the kindness and cruelty she had encountered in Iran. She shuddered at the thought that she could have been locked up in jail, still be there.

So much had been disturbing to her. Even her brief affair with the doctor, though in some ways exciting, had a painful tinge to it, even in retrospect. It seemed more like an act of desperation than anything else.

Finally she fell asleep and then woke to Darius's voice calling, "Mommy." She got out of the bed and went to check on him, but he had been calling in his sleep as he had sometimes in Iran. She stood there and stared at him for a moment in this spacious room, where he lay on his own bed, holding his teddy bear.

When Darius's school started it was easier for both of them. Every morning she took him to school before she went to the department store she had been assigned to decorate. She was using some of the patterns she had absorbed from Iranian tiles, stained glass, and carpets, striking in this otherwise conventional store. The fact that Darius was adjusting well to school and was not asking as frequently, "When's Daddy coming back?" or saying "I miss Daddy, I miss Grandma," and that she was very busy herself, getting positive feedback on her work, alleviated her loneliness somewhat. Darius was making friends at school, and she and Darius had Nancy and Josh too.

She kept trying to reach Karim by phone. On several occasions someone seemed to actually pick up but she could not hear any voices. Once she heard Zohreh's voice but Zohreh could not hear her and she hung up. On and off the phone would ring several times in a row but when she picked it up there was no voice on the other end.

She had written him a succession of letters. The first one was the telegram she sent from Istanbul. ". . . I hope you won't be too upset to find that we've left. I'll call or write as soon as we're home and explain everything. Darius is a little better already, don't worry. My apologies to the family too . . ."

Then she had written him the very next morning after they arrived:

> . . . I've been trying to reach you by phone but, not surprisingly, I've had no luck. Darius is already all better, and except for missing you and his grandmother he's fine. The house is in order and I'm busy getting my work organized and Darius ready for school, but still it's hard for both of us to be here without you. I feel your absence in a huge way. I miss you in bed most of all. It has been so long since we've been in the privacy of our room. I miss your arms around me late at night and the feeling of your body against mine . . .

She had written him again after Darius had been at school for a week.

. . . Darius loves the Juniper Tree School. It turned out to be a good choice. In fact he's thriving there already. . . . I haven't heard from you. It frightens me, what's happening? I never told you about my arrest in Qom . . .

Finally, after over a month, she had a letter from Karim.

. . . I've been trying to reach you by phone too. At first your departure with Darius threw Aziz and me into a panic. I went on a frantic search for you. I found out from the agent at the Turkish Airlines that you had changed your tickets—I must have looked very sad or upset because he was willing to give me that information. Then as soon as I got back home your telegram was waiting for me. . . . We all realized how frightened and upset you must have been to be locked out of the house. How angry you must have been at Aziz for taking Darius away to Qom without asking you—but remember she's an old-fashioned woman. She feels a certain authority with her grandchild. These are misunderstandings that could have easily been ironed out if you had stayed on. . . . It was so sad to see how Darius had lost his vitality, his playful spirit. And it was a pity I had so little time to show him and you around. I was absorbed in my responsibilities toward my family I had neglected for so long. I know you understand. We had an accident on the way to

Babolsar. My uncle had some injuries but luckily he's recovering well. Then, hard to believe, I lost my passport in the frenzy of the accident. Now I'm waiting for a new one. I'm hoping it won't take six months, as they have told me. I've been to the passport office several times pressuring them. I'm trying to make it there for the beginning of the term. If I miss a week or so it won't matter all that much . . .

His next letter said,

. . . How wonderful it would be to just talk to you and Darius. Now I'm aiming to be there no later than December to make sure everything will be smooth for the second semester. Ed wrote a letter, expressing his dismay at my taking a leave of absence. . . . Is there any chance that you and Darius could come back? I know he's adjusting well to his school—that's great news, but I'm sure he would do well at a school here too. He was picking up the language quickly and this time he might be more immune to whatever made him sick last time. I know they value you enough at the company to let you work for them long distance from here, on a freelance basis at least for a while . . .

She could not conceive of the idea of going back to live there. Always under the scrutiny of *pasdars*, a foreigner, she felt she would lose her identity, disappear, the way Karim had felt here.

Would Karim be fired if he didn't come back for the second semester, she wondered? Would he be able to find another job? Would she be able to find something worthwhile if they both had to look for jobs in another city?

At times, in her bewilderment, she thought perhaps it was just as well that Karim was in Iran right now. She could not bear the pain he had felt so much of the time in Athens. She thought again of his saying, "I'm never going to be happy again here," and realized how thin the delineation was between his unhappiness and hers. Every one of his moods and feelings spilled into her.

Weeks passed before she had another letter from him.

> . . . You know how hard it is to just abandon everyone and everything here. My uncle is still weak, not able to go to work, though he was offered a job. I've actually taken on a temporary job here and I love it. I'm working with a team of experts, all hired by a company to reconstruct a small village outside of Teheran, heavily damaged by bombs. The work is so meaningful, not at all abstract like what I was doing at the university there. I know missing one more semester is going to be the final straw for Ed.
> I'll have to look for something elsewhere, that means we'll both have to. I'm still hoping you and Darius will join me here. I want to do things right this time. I want

both of you to have a better time, a good life here. I'm disappointed that you said you can't make the decision to return here so soon. My heart melts thinking of our dear Darius. How sad it is that circumstances have torn me apart from you and my little dear boy but I know the three of us are strong enough to be able to stand the separation as long as it needs to be. I hope you don't feel too alone. That the responsibilities of caring for Darius and so much else aren't too much for you without me sharing them . . .

No, she couldn't go there, at least not for a long time. She had just been given a challenging job to do, designing children's rooms at Athens Hospital, a great chance for her. And Darius was doing better and better.

Often she stared out at the street from the kitchen window and sometimes she saw a fleeting image of Karim returning home on his bicycle, the way he used to. Over the months she prepared a conversation to have with him when he came back and kept revising it as time went by.